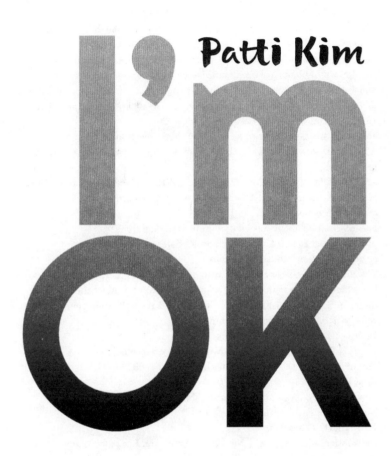

Patti Kim

I'm OK

Atheneum Books for Young Readers

New York London Toronto Sydney New Delhi

ATHENEUM BOOKS FOR YOUNG READERS

atheneum An imprint of Simon & Schuster Children's Publishing Division

1230 Avenue of the Americas, New York, New York 10020

ATHENEUM BOOKS FOR YOUNG READERS is a registered trademark of Simon & Schuster, Inc. Atheneum logo is a trademark of Simon & Schuster, Inc.

For information about special discounts for bulk purchases, please contact Simon & Schuster Special Sales at 1-866-506-1949 or business@simonandschuster.com.

The Simon & Schuster Speakers Bureau can bring authors to your live event. For more information or to book an event, contact the Simon & Schuster Speakers Bureau at 1-866-248-3049 or visit our website at www.simonspeakers.com.

Interior design by Vikki Sheatsley

The text for this book was set in New Century Schoolbook.

Manufactured in the United States of America   0918 FFG

First Edition   10 9 8 7 6 5 4 3 2 1

Library of Congress Cataloging-in-Publication Data

Names: Kim, Patti, 1970– author.

Title: I'm Ok / Patti Kim.

Description: First edition. | New York : Atheneum Books for Young Readers, [2018] | Summary: Ok, a Korean American boy, tries a get rich quick scheme of starting a hair braiding business and winning the school talent competition to hide the fact that he is struggling with the loss of his father and the financial hardships he and his mother must now bear.

Identifiers: LCCN 2017046909 | ISBN 9781534419292 (hardcover) | ISBN 9781534419315 (eBook)

Subjects: | CYAC: Mothers and sons—Fiction. | Korean Americans—Fiction. | Loss (Psychology)—Fiction. | Moneymaking projects—Fiction.

Classification: LCC PZ7.1.K5835 Im 2018 | DDC [Fic]—dc23

LC record available at https://lccn.loc.gov/2017046909

For Ellie and Sophie

one

The woman's face is so close to mine that I can tell her eyebrows aren't real. Doodling in some eyes, fins, and tails would turn the pair into two fish facing off. Her eyes are red from crying. Her cheeks are streaked with gray from mascara that made a run for it. She looks down at me. I sink into my corner seat. There's no place to hide in the basement of the First Korean Full Gospel Church.

"I feel so sorry for you. Poor, poor boy. Poor, poor Ok. What are you going to do? My heart, my heart," she says, slapping her chest with her right hand, which is shackled with golden rings suffocating her plump fingers. "My heart aches for you and your mother," she says, and pounds my back with a force that would dislodge a rock from my throat.

I bow my head and wait for her to move on to the group of women in the middle of the room, huddled around my mother like burrowing wasps, buzzing loud prayers. They moan and babble because the Holy Spirit has a hold of them. I wish the Holy Spirit would get a hold of me so I could wail my sadness too.

As soon as Fish Brows leaves, another woman rushes to me. She squats down at my feet so she can meet my lowered head. She puts her hand on my shoulder, looks up into my eyes, and tells me my father is in heaven, smiling down on me. See him? The woman bids me to be good and strong for my mother and have faith in God's will, because I'm the man of the house now. God works in mysterious ways.

I nod like a robot. She stands and pulls me in to her, pressing my cheek against her stomach. I hear her heart beat, her insides gurgle, and her stomach growl. She opens her purse, digs out her wallet, pulls out bills, stuffs the money into the pockets of my borrowed suit jacket two sizes too big, and tells me to take good care of my mother. What does this mean? Isn't she supposed to take care of me? I politely say thank you.

As Moneybags leaves, another woman walks toward me. She carries a plate of food. She's short and round and looks plenty hungry. I brace myself for baptism by spit and bits of food. The plate is piled high with rice, fried dumplings, grilled short ribs, fried chicken wings, kimchi, bean cakes, potato salad, and japchae noodles. The woman looks down at me, smiles like we know each other, and puts her plate of food on my lap. It smells good. She tells me to eat, eat up, even if I'm not hungry, even if I don't feel like it, because I'm going to need all the strength and energy to grow through this very hard thing that's happened to me. It's not normal, she says. It's all wrong. What a senseless mess. Makes you want to kick some idiot's butt, she says, shaking her head and exhaling, "*Aigo. Aigo.*" I take a bite of rice. It's warm and soft and sticky, and tears start to form in my eyes, and soon my food is being sauced with snot. The woman hands me a napkin, and I thank her. I wipe my face, thinking how much I need my father to come back to life.

two

I help my mother sew. I stand behind her as she's curled over a borrowed sewing machine parked on our dining table. I pin the cuffs to the sleeves and stack them in a pile, waiting for my mother to stitch them. She earns a nickel for every cuff and sleeve she brings together. This is her job at night, after she's cooked in the morning for a carryout called Soul Nice in DC and worked in the afternoon and evening as a cashier at Arirang Grocery. She works without stopping, to make ends meet, to keep us fed, to keep a roof over our heads, to send me to college someday, to keep from missing him, to keep alive my father's plan for success in the USA. In two years, he said, he would buy his dream property, which was the dilapidated house located outside our apartment complex. Fix it up. Live in it. Sell it for a nice profit. In five years he would own his roofing business. In six years he would send me to college. In eight years he would visit Korea.

In ten years he would buy me a car for my graduation.

"Ok-ah," my mother says. "Fix these pins. They're crooked. Pay attention."

As I straighten the pins, I accidentally prick myself. A bead of blood forms on my thumb, and my mother elbows me away, telling me to hurry and go get cleaned up before I stain something, because we can't afford to pay for what gets damaged. The point is to make money, not lose it.

I go to the bathroom. While putting on a Band-Aid, I remember how my mother used to make her own with toilet paper and Scotch tape. She would fold a square down to the size of a quarter and gently use it to cover my wound with two strips of tape. She made such a fuss whenever I got hurt. She'd say, "*Aigo. Aigo.* What have you done to yourself? Hurry, let me take care of it before you bleed to death." Her urgent attention always had a way of making me feel better, even if I was bleeding to death.

I quickly return to help. Once I've backed up my mother with a tower of pinned cuffs and sleeves ready to sew, she says, "Go make some ramen for us."

I go to the kitchen. I've gotten good at cooking ramen. When the water boils, I add the blocks of noodles and soup base. I chop green onions and cut Spam into little cubes. I crack two eggs into the pot, break the yolks, and watch the liquid turn murky. I plop in two scoops of rice and watch the grains swim and separate. My ramen is the best. My father's was pretty good too. He used to melt a slice of American cheese into his, turning the soup creamy. It was very tasty for about two minutes, and then the gas and cramps would kick in. I'm not on friendly terms with lactose.

I set the bowls on the coffee table in the living room because the dining table has turned into a city with skyscrapers of partially assembled shirts. My mother and I sit on the floor. She says grace, and we eat, slurping noodles under the watchful eyes of my father, whose portrait is framed in black and propped on top of the television. Next to him is a shot glass of Johnnie Walker, a Camel cigarette and lighter, a bowl of Starburst candy, a plate of dried squid, and a pyramid of Oreo cookies that shrinks every time I walk by.

"This is so good," my mother says.

I smile, feeling proud.

"Ok-ah, eating your ramen makes me feel like everything's going to be fine. I'm not worried. God will take care of us. We just need to do our part and believe he loves us. Sometimes things don't make sense, but there's so much we don't know, so we have to trust him. No matter what happens, we have to trust him," she says.

I nod, bring the bowl up to my lips, and pour soup into my mouth.

After she eats, my mother sits on the couch and closes her eyes. "For just a minute," she says. I clean up. When I come back from the kitchen, I see her, sitting upright, her hands crossed on her lap, her head tilted to one side, dangling like a sunflower too heavy for its stem. She sleeps.

"Ŏmma," I say. She doesn't answer. I look around the room. The sewing isn't done. They're coming in the morning for pickup. I need to wake her up.

"Ŏmma," I say again, and tap her on the shoulder. My mother falls over, landing on her side, her head hanging off the edge of a cushion. Her mouth is wide open. She snores.

It was a rule never to wake my parents up when they napped after church on Sunday afternoons. I imagined their Sunday best thrown about the room, my father's suit, shirt, and tie deflated at the foot of the bed, and my mother's dress draped over a chair, while they snored. When I was younger, I watched TV, played jacks, rode my Big Wheel back and forth on the balcony, waiting for them to wake up. They always woke up hungry and too groggy to cook anything, so my father would announce dinner at Bob's Big Boy. We'd sit in a booth, me enclosed by my mother to my right, a wall to my left, and my father in front of me. Between sips of his Coke, he told me that I could accomplish anything in this country if I put my mind to it. Opportunities abounded.

I sit in front of the Singer, wondering, How hard can it be? Working a sewing machine can't be as hard as making the best ramen. I take off my T-shirt and use it to practice. Press pedal with foot. The harder you press, the faster the needle pumps. Guide the fabric through like you're feeding the hungry needle. *Chomp-chomp.* It's a cinch. I sew my first cuff to a sleeve. It looks good. A nickel earned. *Ka-ching.* I sew my second pair, then a third. I'm on a roll. The sewing machine hums. I complete the pile. The point is to make money, not lose it. *Ka-ching.* I want my mother to wake up and see what I've accomplished for her, but she snores.

I wash up, go to bed, and sleep.

I dream that I'm running through a field with Clifford the Big Red Dog, except he's not as big as he appears in the books. He's the more reasonable size of a horse, rather than a house. And Emily Elizabeth is there too, running with us. She's very cute, and she keeps calling me Charley, but I don't mind. We play fetch. We laugh. We ride on Clifford's back. We feed him apples. It's all perfect and happy, like a dog-food commercial, until Clifford starts to bark. He barks and barks and barks and won't stop. Then he growls and growls and growls and growls. His growling wakes me up, and I slowly realize it's not Clifford, it's the sound of the sewing machine.

My mother shouldn't be sewing. There's nothing left to sew. I finished it all. I get out of bed to see what's going on.

I stand in the dark hall. My mother doesn't notice me. She's hunched over the machine, its needle pumping thread through fabric. The jelly-bean-size bulb lights her face. She picks up a set from the pile I sewed, takes a seam ripper, and pulls apart my stitching. My stomach sinks. I did it all wrong. I made things worse. I made more work for her. I feel so sorry. I feel so stupid. She turns the cuff, rearranges it against the sleeve, and sews it correctly. I return to my room and crawl back into bed. I stare up at the ceiling. I knuckle my head twelve times, for each year I've been alive, mumbling, *"pabo, pabo, pabo, pabo,"* just as my father would've done. Don't call me stupid. My name is Ok. At least I didn't trip while working on a roof and come tumbling down and land so hard and wrong on concrete that my neck broke. I'm sorry. I'm sorry. I knuckle my head again. They said he died instantly. They said he felt nothing. No pain.

I feel the springs of the mattress against my back. The barley grains inside my pillow cradle my head. The blanket warms my cold feet. The moonlight casts a shadow of the tree outside my bedroom window. Its dangling leaves make me wish money grew on trees.

three

No one sits at the front of the school bus, so that's where I go, right behind Mr. Rufus, with his black leather driving gloves, mirrored aviator sunglasses, and the shoulders of a defensive lineman. I don't mind being alone up here. I prefer it. It's not so bumpy, which decreases my chances of getting carsick and throwing up. Cannot risk throwing up. I can also hear the faint sound of Mr. Rufus's radio, which plays classical music. And most importantly, I'm far from the likes of Asa Banks, who sits with his own personal audience and portable fan club in the back of the bus, making an annoying ruckus—you know, the typical sounds friends make when having fun. Asa and I had a run-in some time ago, and I try to avoid him at all costs.

It happened in the hall. I was on my way to the boys' bathroom but stopped to stare at the poster hanging above the water fountain, about the upcoming talent contest. The prize would be a hundred big ones. All interested students should sign up at the front office. One hundred dollars up for grabs? Sign me up! My eyes were getting wide, seeing the earning potential, when Asa, coming from the opposite way, looked at me. I failed to turn away in time, and our eyes met. A split second of eye contact was all he needed to let loose on me. I stared at my feet and prayed I wouldn't piss my pants, prayed I wouldn't get beat up because I looked like one of those kids you couldn't help but beat up. If you were big, bad, and bored, you were going to want to use me as a punching bag, or worse, a urinal. Something about me embodied the ideal victim. Something about being Korean, about having hair that grew out like a Chia Pet's, about my big, block-shaped head, my buck-teeth, my slit eyes, the archipelago of acne on my chin, forehead, and right cheek, my cracking voice, my use of words like "archipelago," and my impeccable grades made people want to squash me like an annoying cockroach.

"Boo!" Asa said, stopping in front of me.

I froze. He smelled my fear. He leaned down into my face. He was close, any closer and my hair-needles would've pricked his eyes. I avoided his stare and looked at his mouth. His lips were plump. The top lip was brown. The lower lip was pink. Spit lined them, and when he opened his mouth to speak, stalagmites and stalactites formed. Asa burped loud and long in my face. It came from deep within, because I smelled his baloney sandwich from two days ago. I threw up in my mouth and swallowed it back down to keep from messing up his Nikes. He had nice sneakers. He wore perfectly creased jeans that fell at just the right place on his Nikes. Next to his feet, mine in their used knockoff Chucks from Value Thrift looked like they belonged to a poor toddler. My jeans were too short and showed some sock. It was a rule among the cool kids at Landover Hills Middle to never show sock.

"Nice socks, Okie Dorkie," Asa said.

No one at school said my name right. It's Ok. Try this: Say "pork." Drop the p sound. Now drop the r sound. Ok. I'd been kind of wanting to test this out, but everyone ended up calling me Oak, like the tree, which I'd gotten used to. At least it conjured up images of something big and strong. But Asa couldn't even give me the benign mispronunciation. He went for the jugular. Okie Dorkie. That was a good one.

I stared at the third button on his shirt and said nothing.

"I said, nice socks."

I said nothing.

"In this country, when you get a compliment, you say 'thank you.' You know what a compliment is, boy?"

he asked, wrapping his hand around the top of my head. He grabbed my hair and shook my head up and down, forcing me to nod. He held back my head like a Pez dispenser and said, "You sure about that? Well, I don't think you know what a compliment is, 'cause if you did, you'd be saying 'thank you' to me 'cause I told you a compliment by telling you how nice your socks show, but you didn't say nothing back to me, so I'm feeling like you trying to disrespect me and hurt my feelings or something. You trying to hurt my feelings?" With a handful of my hair, he shook my head left and right. "So what you suppose to say when someone give you a compliment?"

I said nothing. I looked down, staring at that third button on his shirt. It was round and white with four holes and was held in place by yellow thread. The others were sewn on with white thread. Perfect white X marks holding the buttons in their places, but the third button was all messed up. Someone had done a lousy sewing job. Instead of an X, the button was held in place by an incomplete square, a three-sided should've-been-an-X. Asa, dressed in jeans with sharp creases along the sides, a shirt with sharp creases along the sleeves, and Nikes, had a mother who didn't know how to sew.

"What'd I tell you? Why you be so rude? You deaf? You speak English? Wong-chung-chung?" Asa said, poking me in the chest with the corner of the hall pass. Three pokes. One for each syllable.

I cleared my throat, put my hands together like I was praying, stuck out my buckteeth, squinted my eyes, bowed, and said, "Okay. Okay. Wong-chung-chung. You happy now?"

Asa let go of my head, slapped his leg, and laughed with his mouth wide open and his teeth showing white and bright, like a toothpaste commercial.

I tried my best not to break into a run and limp-strutted back to the classroom, scared and nervous, expecting Asa to jump me from behind. I was nothing but a traitor with a full bladder. I betrayed someone or something in me. Here was the mark of a true coward: making fun of the way your own mother talked to give your enemy a good laugh. What a loser.

My head bops against the bus window as I try to think of ways not to be a loser. I need to bring in a regular income for my household like my father used to do. I could earn a hundred dollars by winning that school talent show, but I have no talent, not the kind they're looking for. Hearing violins cry from Mr. Rufus's radio, I wish I played an instrument. Maybe I could sing and dance for the talent show? Do my Michael Jackson impersonation? They would definitely boo me off the stage. Magic tricks? Telling jokes? Juggling? As

15

Mr. Rufus turns the steering wheel like he's stirring a big pot of soup, the bus enters Parkside Gardens and rolls over a speed bump, causing the kids in the back to exaggerate their bounce and say woo. They burst out laughing. They're not laughing at me, I assure myself, fighting my curiosity to turn and look.

I almost never laugh at school. But I do remember this one time I couldn't stop laughing. It was last year. I was placed into this advanced reading group called Booked, and we were talking about revenge in *Island of the Blue Dolphins*, and this one girl, her name was Carole, she was very serious and proper and had perfect manners, she sneezed really hard, so hard that she farted at the same time, and it had all of us dead silent, staring at one another. When the teacher said, "Bless you," we all burst out hysterically laughing. Carole even laughed , trying to say thank you. It was the one time I felt like myself in school. After that incident it was like ice had broken, and we all participated more during discussions. This one kid named Jerome even told us about his grandfather, who went to jail for marching for civil rights with Martin Luther King Jr. I even shared how reading books was sometimes the only thing that kept me from feeling like a complete outsider, and they all nodded in agreement. They don't have Booked in middle school.

I scramble out of the bus. I walk quickly, avoiding anyone who might be noticing me and trying to catch up to ask about homework or an upcoming test or something like that, not that that's ever happened, but I like taking precautions. I hurry to vanish from the scene. Invisibility is key to survival. If you're invisible, you don't get in trouble. You don't get hurt. No one sees you. No one at school knows about what happened to my dad. Not even the teachers. My mother said they didn't need to know, since I didn't miss any school days. My mother said I don't need people feeling sorry for me, especially my teachers. The pity of a teacher poisons judgment and contaminates the learning process.

As I walk to our apartment building, I see Dolores Brades on her patio, braiding a woman's hair. Our downstairs neighbor wears fancy high-heel boots, leather pants, and a leopard-print sweater. I stare as she braids, her long red nails flashing among the dark strands of hair. I hear Dolores showing off about her fancy Camaro. If I had her car, I'd show off too. It's sapphire blue and shines like diamonds.

I know her name because taped to her door is a sign that reads DOLORES BRADES, with her phone number in red marker.

What's puzzling is that her mailbox, which is right next to ours, has Olarunfemi as her last name. As I get closer to them, it dawns on me: Dolores can't spell. Dolores Olarunfemi braids hair for money. If fancy-car-fancy-clothes-fancy-shoes-fancy-nails Dolores, who cannot properly spell what she does for money, can do it, so can I.

"Good afternoon, Mrs. Olarunfemi," I say, walking by her.

"Mrs.? Who call me Mrs.? I am no Mrs. No man be owning me. I am Miss. Miss O. Like O for Oprah," she says, laughing into the braid between her fingers.

"My apologies, Miss O," I say, and stand there, staring at her fingers.

"Hey, little mister, how you know my name? You my little stalker?" she says. Her customer laughs. Miss O chuckles. Keeping her eyes on the braid, she says, "You stare long enough, I be charging you by the minute, you know."

I hurry into our building and dash up the steps with an idea and violins playing in my head.

four

I sit under a poster for the upcoming talent show in the back corner of the cafeteria and eat alone, wondering if competitive eating could be considered a talent. I could eat a hundred hot dogs for one hundred dollars. I'd eat bugs for a hundred dollars. People love watching things that gross them out. I open my can of sardines. I don't mind eating alone. I read two books. The one on the outside came highly recommended by my social studies teacher, Ms. Lincoln, about Andy Rusch, a boy my age who has a weirdo friend who eats an excessive amount of onions like they're apples. I like onions, so I can relate. The book I'm hiding inside *Onion John* is an instructional manual on how to braid hair. Peering over my books, I see Asa and his entourage limp-strut into the cafeteria. I've practiced that walk at home. I haven't quite perfected it yet. My mother watched me limp-strut from the sewing machine to the kitchen and asked if my leg was hurt.

"No," I said.

"Then don't walk like that," she said.

It was the walk of the Asas of the world, the walk of the big and the bad. It was the walk of men like Clint Eastwood. My father loved that man. Whenever he pointed at me with hands shaped like pistols, he was trying to be Clint. Whenever he squinted, he was trying to be Clint. Whenever he chose silence or mumbled, or walked stiff like he couldn't bend his knees, or let his cigarette barely hang on to the ledge that was his lower lip, he was trying to be Clint. I get it. This wanting to talk some other talk and walk some other walk that says I own this cafeteria, I own this classroom, I own this bus, I own you.

What makes Asa look like he owns the world makes me look lame.

"Anyone sitting here?" Mickey McDonald asks, standing beside me with a tray.

Mickey's nickname is Old McDonald, not because she has a farm or anything, but because she wears old clothes, like corduroy bell-bottoms and velour shirts with collars big enough for Dracula. I've seen the popular girls tease her. Mickey instructs them that it's vintage, it's disco chic, and the girls hold their noses as they say, "Ewww. Don't talk to us. Out of the way, Mothballs."

Mickey stands near me, wearing a Bee Gees T-shirt.

Her hair is big, like atomic-bomb-mushroom-cloud big, and my fingers twitch, wanting to practice the fine art of braiding. She smells like bug spray, but it doesn't bother me.

"Yeah," I say, angling my books over my food.

"Who?" she asks. "Your imaginary friends that eat with you every day?"

"Sure," I say.

"Liar," she says.

"Medusa," I say.

"A muh-what?" she says.

I want her to take the seat so that I can tell her all about how Medusa, who was supposed to be like a virgin nun for Athena, fell for Poseidon, the god of the sea, and married him. If you had a chance at marrying the sea god, wouldn't you? But this ticked Athena off so badly that she cursed Medusa with green skin and snakes for hair. Talk about eternal damnation. Green skin, snakes for hair, and if you made eye contact, she turned you to stone.

"Ching-chong," Mickey says.

"Ping-pong," I say.

"Ding-dong," she says, and stomps away.

Who needs to eat with other people? It's not so bad alone. I prefer eating by myself. Leave me alone with my ching-chong cuisine of stinky fish cakes, kimchi, candied fish, pickled radish, mandu, bulgogi, and kimbap. There's nothing like opening up that wrinkled, used-one-too-many-times, about-to-rip-apart aluminum foil and finding kimbap in three neat rows stacked two layers deep like Legos and smelling oh so stinky. Rice, Spam, egg, dandelion leaves, pickled radish, and carrots rolled up in seaweed. Yum. I wouldn't trade it for company with the VIP of Landover Hills.

Once, I packed my own lunch, a cheese sandwich on white bread with potato chips and an apple, thinking maybe someone would sit next to me, or the new contents of my lunch might give me the confidence to plop myself down next to a person of my choosing, but it didn't work. I ate alone. The only difference was that the food was lousy, and minutes later my stomach was cramping because I'm lactose intolerant. The cheese made me churn. I was also starving and ended up wasting my emergency quarters on a bag of Fritos that had only five chips in it. Rip-off.

I don't buy school lunch, although I'd probably qualify for reduced lunch, but I think my mother is too proud to sign me up for it. She says that that food is no good and will make me sick and stupid. So I learned my lesson: Eat Ŏmma's food to keep from becoming sick, stupid, and poor.

And for the record, we're not poor. It's just that my

mother is frugal. Ways my mother likes to save money: reuse aluminum foil and plastic bags; flush the toilet once a day; use public restrooms as much as possible; bring home toilet paper, paper towels, and soap from public restrooms; fill her pockets with napkins, straws, and packets of ketchup, mustard, salt, pepper, sugar, and cream from McDonald's; keep lights off; cut each other's hair; hang clothes to dry; shop at thrift stores; buy marked-down food at the grocery store; gather acorns to make acorn gelatin (actually, this is really tasty); eat weeds like dandelion and nettle; grow food on our balcony; and collect rainwater.

Let's put this in perspective, as Ms. Lincoln would say. Maybe by American standards we're a little poor, but by the whole world's standards we're not. We have indoor plumbing. Back in Korea, I got potty trained in an outhouse. My mother used to tell me horror stories of children falling into the pit of poop. We have electricity, clothes on our backs, shoes on our feet, meals every day, free education. In Korea, schools aren't free. Everyone has to pay tuition, and you have to bribe the teachers regularly so they don't mistreat your kids. We have a car (but Ŏmma doesn't have a driver's license), a television set, and toilet paper. I don't have to use newspapers to clean my butt. (Some still do that in Korea. That's why kids run around with ink-stained butts.) I don't have to use my left hand. (Some still do that in India. That's why you're not supposed to eat with your left hand or extend it to anyone as a greeting. Big insult because you're basically telling them to shake your poo-poo hand.)

We're not poor. We might not have as much money as we did when my father was alive, but we're not poor. Sometimes my mother buys meat, not the feet, tongue, or nose of an animal, but real meat. That's not poor. With my father gone, there's one less mouth to feed. No more Camels. No more Johnnie Walker. No more secondhand smoke. No more ashes. No more TV on all night wasting electricity. More savings for us. We're better off. I'll bet he was with Johnnie Walker on that roof. I'll bet he was smoking, too. I'll bet he lost his balance trying to keep his cigarette from falling off his lower lip. Blaming him helps. I don't miss him. I don't. I have everything under control.

The bell rings. Lunch is over. As I get up to throw away my trash, I see Asa shooting a spork into Mickey's hair. It sticks on the back like a dart to a board. She can't even feel it. Asa's friends point and laugh. Some girl giggles and says, "Oh my God, that's so mean," but does nothing about it. Another girl says, "Someone's hungry for attention." Some other girl says, "Her hair is, like, so huge. Big girl, big hair."

As I walk by them, I shake my head. It stinks to be teased. I know what that's like, and I feel sorry for Mickey. I want to say something smooth and heroic like, "Yeah, she is a big girl, big in the best sense of the word, but you, on the other hand, are nothing but small minded, feeble brained, and too blind to see that your own hair is a regular grease pit. When was the last time you shampooed? Shampoo more often. And you know what would look beautiful on you? Braids. You should treat yourself to some pretty braids to crown that pretty little head of yours. Here's my business card. The name is Ok. Get braided by Ok."

But I don't say anything. I lower my head and leave the cafeteria, hurrying to catch up to Mickey. As I quietly walk behind her, I reach up, quickly pull the spork out of her hair, and make a run for it around the corner.

five

While my mother is at work, I watch TV at home. A commercial comes on. A man wearing a blue suit jacket, white shirt, and red tie looks at me. He's bald, with bushy eyebrows shaped like baby Snickers bars. His cheeks are pink. His forehead bubbles up with beads of sweat like small blisters after a burn. He's serious. He's upset. He's important.

His mustache twitches, trying to hang on as his words shoot out of his mouth: "Have you been hurt? Have you been in an accident? Have you been injured on the job through no fault of your own? Well, you need a lawyer who will fight for you. Get what you deserve. I can get you fast cash settlements. Call me, Trent Bedderman. I'm the man for the job. I won't stand for injustice. You have rights. And I'll do everything in my power to get what's rightfully yours. When things are looking down, look me up. Trent Bedderman. Because you deserve the best."

I turn off the TV. I sit on the floor in the dimming light, surrounded by my mother's sewing. My father's portrait looks down at me. It's an enlarged black-and-white of his passport picture, so he looks young. His slicked-back hair is stiff with gel. His skin is smooth and pale, which is not what he really looked like. He had a tan. He had stubble. He had wrinkles around his eyes, which deepened when he smiled. I remember because he didn't smile a lot. The look in his eyes tee-ters between fear and courage. I remember that look. I saw it often. Depending on how I felt, it either scared or emboldened me.

I open my backpack. As I take out my math book, the class picture order form falls out. Picture day is tomor-row. I need a check to order pictures of myself. Last year my parents ordered a package that cost eighteen dol-lars. I guess I won't be ordering pictures this year. Not a big deal. I'll ask to go to the bathroom when Ms. Lincoln passes them out. Besides, I haven't changed that much. I open to page 62. How to calculate the area of circles. I start on my homework.

I'm hungry.

My mother won't be home for five hours. The rice maker is turned off, which means there's no rice. I'd bet-ter make some before she gets home. We keep the rice grains in a big plastic barrel under the sink. I open the lid. There's only about a cup left. I pour every single grain into the rice maker and leave the barrel out to show my mother she needs to buy another big sack. This is enough for tonight, but we'll need more tomorrow. I wash the grains. The water is murky white at first. With each rinse, the water clears. I drop the bowl into the rice maker and push the on button.

Our fridge is practically empty. Three eggs, a brown banana, a slice of Spam, an orange juice carton half full of barley tea. The bottom shelf holds four large jars of kimchi, which I can't touch because they're reserved for selling to some deacons at church. My mother makes the best kimchi. The church ladies want to know her secret. She lies, tells them it's raw oysters you need, it's more garlic, it's pears, it's her homegrown red peppers. The women complain it doesn't work. My mother tells them to lay their hands on the batch and pray. It never works. She won't give her secret away. It's bad for business.

When my mother makes kimchi, our apartment reeks of garlic, but it's okay because the four big jars of her kimchi lined up in the fridge give me hope for a better future.

I look in the pantry. Ramen noodles. I grab a pack. I put some water on to boil.

The phone rings.

"Hello," I answer.

"Oh, who is this?" the man says. I can tell he's Korean from his accent.

"Hello," I answer in Korean.

"Is your mother there?" the man asks in Korean.

"I'm sorry, but no, she's not here," I say.

"Then can you tell me when she'll be home?"

"She'll be home later. Excuse me, but may I ask who's calling, please?"

"Oh. Yes, this is Deacon Koh from church. You must be Ok. How are you doing?"

"I'm doing fine," I say.

"How's school coming along?"

"School is fine," I say.

"How are your grades?"

"They're fine," I say.

"Uh, I'm just calling to see if you and your mother are doing all right," he says, sounding nervous and fishy. His voice doesn't sound like this is just a courtesy phone call on behalf of the church. Deacon Koh is known as the lonely widower of FKFGC, and I've seen him trying to talk to my mother during fellowship hour after service.

"Hello, Deacon Koh. We're fine. I'll let her know she received a call from church."

"Uh, tell her it's Deacon Koh."

"I will. Thank you. Good-bye," I say, and hang up.

The water on the stove boils. The phone rings again. I let it ring because I suspect it's the deacon again, wanting to leave his personal phone number. But then again, it could be my mother calling to ask me if she needs to bring home a new sack of rice. It could also maybe be Jerome from Booked. We're in the same science class. I answer it.

"Good evening. This is Pepco calling. Am I speaking with Mr. Lee?" The woman's voice is clear, confident, and full of purpose, like a teacher's voice calling roll. *Mr. Lee? Is there a Mr. Lee present? Raise your hand and say "Here."*

It's easier for me to answer yes, so I deepen my voice, turn on my Korean accent, and say, "Speaking."

"Mr. Lee, I'm calling to notify you that your Pepco bill in the amount of fifty-nine dollars and seventy cents is three months overdue. If you cannot pay this amount in full by the next due date, we will have to shut off your electricity. You will lose your power, Mr. Lee. Do you understand?"

"Yes. Yes. I understand. I take care. I take care. Thank you berry, berry much," I say, and hang up, my heart pounding hard.

The water boils over. I turn down the heat, carefully drop the noodles in, and watch the dry block soften and separate. What was once stiff and brittle comes unglued. The curls relax into waves as the noodles depart from one another. I sprinkle in the soup base, and the water browns. My mouth waters as I stir the noodles and wonder how in the world Trent Bedderman might get us some cash. Fast.

six

My mother and I are at church. We sit in the back pew. Pastor Chung finishes his sermon by telling us to bow our heads in prayer.

I close my eyes and pray, telling God that I need a talent for the talent show so I can win a hundred dollars, and that I want Deacon Koh to get married so my mother doesn't get any ideas, and that I want Miss O to teach me how to braid so that we can have fancy things too, but I know she won't. It's bad for her business. The point is to make money, not lose it. I've gone to the library and checked out a book called *Be Your Own Boss: Easy Steps to Starting a Small Business*. I know the steps by heart.

Step #1: Brainstorm types of skills that fit your interests.
(I am interested in making money. I am interested in making the world more beautiful. I can combine my interests in making money and making beauty by

braiding hair. I don't have any braiding skills yet, but I have a book that can teach me. I am a fast learner. I am good with my hands. My braiding skills will pave the way to big bucks.)

Step #2: Research competitors and how much they charge.
(Dolores charges sixty dollars for three hours of braiding. That's a lot of money. Enough to pay our overdue electric bill with change left over. No one else braids at my church or school. Unbraided territories. There's potential for a monopoly here.)

Step #3: Write down a business plan.
(My business plan is to make money braiding hair. I plan on charging fifteen dollars for one braiding session, which is 75 percent less than my competitor. I plan on offering six basic kinds of braids: the French braid, the Dutch braid, the fishtail braid, the Swiss braid, the crown braid, and the microbraid. Well, I might not offer the microbraid, which is what Dolores does on her patio. It takes a long time. Like three to four hours. I figure that if I can do a French braid in fifteen minutes and make fifteen dollars, it's more profitable for me to do four French braids and earn sixty dollars in one hour than the same amount in three hours.)

Step #4: Make a list of initial expenses.

BOOKS FOR RESEARCH: $0. (Get all books free from the library. Remember to return them on time.)

PAPER FOR FLYERS: $0. (Use the back side of all the junk mail we get.)

BUSINESS CARDS: $0. (Take a stack of Pastor Chung's business cards from the church office. If I glue paper over them, I can write my name and number on them. It's okay. No one takes those cards. I've seen some thrown out in the parking lot. Besides, my mother tithes. As far as I'm concerned, she paid for some of those cards.)

PERMANENT MARKER: $0. (Borrow one of Ms. Lincoln's Sharpie markers. She has a box full of them on her desk.)

TAPE: $0. (Use Ms. Lincoln's tape. She keeps rolls of masking tape in her supply closet.)

TIME: $0. (Set up appointments during my free time before school, during lunch and recess, after school, and on weekends and holidays.)

PRIDE: $0. (Braiding hair is not going to look cool. But a man has to do what a man has to do. I must socially prepare myself. My manhood will be brought into question. But what greater duty does a man have than to provide for his family? And I'll get to touch girls. How many boys at school get to touch girls and get paid for it? And the girls will like me for making their hair look so beautiful. Who needs boys when you can have a flock of girls following you around with cash in hand? I must focus on the money. I must press on toward the goal to win the prize. Philippians 3:14.)

Step #5: Get money to cover initial expenses.
(Since my initial expenses amount to $0, skip this step and go on to the next.)

Step #6: Design advertisements and business cards.
(My flyer.)

Do you want to be beautiful?
Do you want to be pretty?
Do you want to be popular?
If yes is your answer,
GET BRAIDED BY OK.
Call 555-6627.
Don't delay! Treat yourself today!

*[Place a picture of Medusa with crazy,
unruly snake hair here and label it "Before."]*

*[Place a picture of Medusa with the same head of snakes
but braided nice and neatly here and label it "After."]*

(My business card.)

Step #7: Tell people about your business.

(Hang flyers on the church bulletin board and at school. Braid the hair of the most popular girl in church: Mi Young Kim. Braid the hair of the most popular girl in my class: Cassandra Cruz. Offer them a one-time free braiding session, because if they get their hair done by Ok, every girl will want it too. Mi Young and Cassandra will spread the word. Word of mouth is the best advertisement. They'll tell two friends, and they'll tell two friends, and so on and so on. I'll be known as the braid-meister, the braidiac, the braid whiz. Appointments will have to be booked weeks in advance. They'll fight over me. *Girls, girls, I only have two hands.* Once demand is high and supply is low, charge more.)

Step #8: Keep track of your money.

(During all my seven years of schooling, I've earned nothing but As in math. I'm in the advanced math class with seventh and some eighth graders. I think I can keep track of my money. During my first week open for business, I anticipate one appointment. I'm keeping my expectations low. It's the secret to happiness. It prevents disappointment, depression, and failure. One appointment means fifteen dollars. During the second week I expect two appointments. By then Cassandra and Mi Young will have spread the word. Two appointments means thirty dollars. That's a lot of money. During the third week I think it's reasonable to predict three appointments, which means forty-five dollars. By the end of my first month, I can make over one hundred dollars.

(Underestimation is fine, but I do need to prepare myself for possible exponential growth. Whatever money I earn, I first give to my mother to help pay rent and bills. Once the basics are taken care of, I can treat myself. I want new jeans. I want new shoes. I want Nikes, the goddess of victory on my feet. I want a real haircut from a real barber. No more Ŏmma cutting my hair with her sewing scissors. I want the deluxe fifty-five-dollar school picture package with the two eight-by-tens and, like, hundreds of those wallet-size photos of me with my new professionally cut head of hair. I can glue those onto my business cards. I want to take my mother out to a fancy restaurant where we can order steak. I want my own private jet. I'll fly us to Korea, where we can show off to our family how rich we are, all because of me. I want a bicycle. I want sunglasses like the ones Mr. Rufus wears. I want a violin. I want a dog.)

Keeping my head lowered, I open my eyes. My pants are too short. Socks show. My fake Chucks are too tight. The duct tape covering the holes from the inside is starting to peel off. If only money grew like I do. If only we could keep up with each other. For every inch, twenty dollars. For every pound, a fifty. Then I wouldn't eye the cash on the offering plate that's coming my way. Lead me not into temptation. As I hold the offering plate, I sniff the bills and hesitate before passing it along.

seven

We're moving from our two-bedroom on Sixty-Fourth to a one-bedroom on Sixty-Eighth. The apartment has the same layout, same balcony, is within the same Parkside Gardens complex, but minus a bedroom, minus the view of the creek, and minus one hundred dollars on rent. We're higher up, moving from the second floor to the third. I guess you can say we're moving up in the world. It's a shorter walk to the bus stop. The place smells like Clorox. The view is of a parking lot.

I can feel the walls closing in on me. My world shrinks. But my mother says we have to do this. We have to save money. We need money, money, money. It's either this or no electricity or no telephone or no three meals. That hundred-dollar prize for winning the talent show would come in handy just about now.

She also sold my father's 1972 Mercury Cougar XR7 to the eager Deacon Koh, the church widower who's crazy about fellowshipping with my mother. He has skin that's cratered like the moon. He has beady eyes. His first wife died in Korea. Cause of death is unknown. His second wife died in America a couple of years ago. Cause of death was cancer. He doesn't have any children. He's got "desperate for a wife" wallpapered all over him. He's on the hunt for wife number three. He's rich. Depending on whom you're eavesdropping on, he's either a businessman or a life insurance agent. No one knows for sure, and no one bothers to investigate because he gives money to the church and does a lot, like sing in the choir and play the guitar and count the offering money and give rides to old people and fellowship with the widows. I smell a crook. I've noticed him offering my mother coffee. Hey, creep, she doesn't drink coffee. He tries to strike up a conversation about the sermon and the weather. He tries to talk to her about the stages of grief and feeling your feelings and letting go and moving on. I guess he talked her into selling my father's car. Or she talked him into buying it. She hated that car.

My father loved that old car. It was the green of the grass that grows on the White House lawn. It had a white vinyl top that matched the white driving cap he wore to hide his thinning hair. I was with him the night he picked it up from Pete's Garage. Just the two of us taking care of the manly business of buying an antique car. He refused to call it used. It was antique. It was historical. I stood behind my father as he offered the long-haired Pete, who had hands as tarred up as his own, a wad of cash for a set of keys. He drove it home with the windows down, with me riding next to him on the passenger side. The seat cradled me. I was too low and couldn't see much of what was outside, but I didn't even try to hang out the window or edge myself up for a better view, because I wanted to stay close to my dad. His right hand shifted gears. His left hand palmed the steering wheel. His feet pumped the pedals as if in some dance. He was free and in control and driving toward possibilities. He didn't smile, just as Clint would never have smiled, but he looked happy, like things were finally going his way. I nestled into the passenger seat, feeling every vibration and jerk, and committed my father's new mood to memory.

If my mother would learn to drive, we could have kept the car. But she refuses. I tell her that driving would make her free. No more waiting for buses or catching cabs or walking in the rain or running late or hitchhiking or begging for rides. She could go to the store whenever she wanted. But she won't learn, not after what happened before. Once upon a time, my father did try to teach her how to drive. She had even gotten her learner's permit. She was practicing at the Safeway parking lot. She thought the car was in reverse, but it wasn't. She ran into a parked car, smashing its headlight. My father called her an idiot, yelled at her, took over the wheel, and raced out of there like it was a getaway. Hit and run. She cried. He told her to shut up. I crouched on the floor of the backseat, scared my mother would get kicked out of the country.

I can see why she'd wanted to get rid of my father's car. Sure, we need the money, but that Cougar was a sore reminder of how my father had belittled her and how she'd failed.

"You take the bedroom," my mother says, unpacking a box in the kitchen.

"No, I like it here," I say, and sit down on my mattress in the dining area.

"Don't be crazy. A son needs his own room," she says, and blows her nose. I think she's crying.

"I do have my own room. I have all this to myself. Besides, I like being next to the kitchen, and I like having the TV right here. This is the best," I say.

"No, it's not," she says, turning on the faucet.

"Ŏmma, it's okay. This is good," I say.

"How can you say this is good? This is bad. This is bad. I feel so sorry," she says.

"No, don't feel sorry. This isn't bad. This is better.

This is much better than the other place," I say, bouncing on the mattress.

"You're throwing up dust. Don't bounce," she says.

"It smells better here," I say, and stop bouncing.

"It smells like a hospital."

"It's brighter. You were always complaining about how dark it was over on that side. We're on the bright side now," I say.

She wipes the countertop, not saying anything, her back to me. I push the mattress into the corner and start unpacking my trash bag of stuff. My mother throws the sponge into the sink, rushes to the bathroom, and shuts the door. She's sad. She's crying. I don't know what to do. I go to the kitchen, pick up the sponge, and finish cleaning the counter. I check the phone for a dial tone. It works. I switch the light on and off. It works. I check the dead bolt on the door. It works. I slide open the balcony door, step out, and slide it shut. It works.

The air outside is crisp and sharp. The sun shines. I lean over the railing and look out at the parking lot. Three kids play basketball with a hoop made from a bottomless bucket tied to a sign. They could use one more player to even the teams out. Maybe I can play.

Who am I kidding? I can't play basketball. I tried shooting hoops with my father once, and I couldn't make a single basket. I was too short. My father told me that you don't have to be tall to play well on a team. Make up for it with speed. All you need to do is get the ball to the tall kid who can shoot. I don't know if anyone would want me on his team.

I hear barking. I look down. On the balcony below ours sits a big dog, staring up at me. He's brown with black spots and looks just like Scooby Doo. I smile and wave, wondering if he might help me solve the mystery of the missing father. His tail wags, as if welcoming me to the building.

eight

Ms. Lincoln stands at the board, telling the class to "put the correct em-PHA-sis on the correct syl-LA-ble." We chuckle. The school secretary's voice chimes into the room through the intercom. "Ms. Lincoln, can you send Oak Lee down to the office? The principal wants to have a talk."

"Awwww," the class says.

"Will do," the teacher says, then looks at me and nods.

This is the first time I've been called to the principal's office. I walk quickly. Sweaty palms. Accelerated heart rate. Heavy breathing. I'm in trouble. The hall is empty and quiet. The glossy, bloodred cinder-block walls make me think of the flames of hell, where there shall be non-stop weeping and gnashing of teeth for all of eternity. The water fountain cycles on. The GET BRAIDED BY OK flyer I taped above the fountain is gone. Two plus two equals four. This summoning has something to do with my braiding business.

"Good afternoon, Ms. Bierman," I say, stepping into the main office. The place smells of Enjoli, the eight-hour perfume for the twenty-four-hour woman. I know exactly how it smells because I sprayed it on myself at Peoples Drug Store. The free-sample bottle had a sticker on it that said TRY ME. So I did. I reeked of Enjoli all day long.

"Hello there, Oak! And how are you today?" she says.

"Fine, thank you. And you?"

"I'm fine too. You can go right in, dear. She's expecting you."

I step into the principal's office. Without looking up from the important papers she's signing with her fancy silver pen, Mrs. Farmer says, "Go ahead and shut the door." I shut the door.

The light in her office is nothing like the light that the fluorescent tubes give off in the rest of the school building. On her desk stands a lamp that casts a soft spotlight over her work, leaving the rest of the room in shadows. It's soap-opera light, the kind of dimness people get all romantic in. It's supposed to be calming and relaxing, but it has the opposite effect on me. I'm nervous like I'm being chugged up a roller coaster. I've never ridden one before, but I've seen enough of them on TV to know I hate roller coasters.

"Sit down," she says. I sit down.

Principal Farmer is the exact opposite of her secretary. While Ms. Bierman is plump and soft, exuding permissiveness and generosity, Mrs. Farmer is thin and hard. She isn't going to put up with any of your nonsense. I wonder if she wears No nonsense panty hose. She certainly doesn't wear Enjoli perfume, although she looks like the twenty-four-hour woman, with the framed college diploma hanging behind her, along with pictures of her husband, kids, and dog back there in the shadows. Bet she has a nice house. Everyone knows she drives a nice car. Her shiny black Cadillac is parked in the designated principal's space. Principal Farmer is a real twenty-four-hour woman, and she doesn't need some eight-hour perfume to make her feel like one. If Mrs. Farmer has a fragrance, it's the smell of a yardstick. She smells like a yardstick and has all the functions of one: to measure, threaten, and punish.

"What is this all about?" she says, looking up at me. She puts down her fancy silver pen and picks up my flyers, all five copies of them.

"I'm sorry," I say. The magic words of appeasement to get me out of here fast. Standard response when you're in trouble. Don't say too much. Like in an

47

interrogation room. Should I ask for a lawyer? Where's Trent Bedderman when you need him?

"It won't happen again. I promise," I say.

"Can you answer my question?"

"I'm sorry, but what was the question again?"

"What is this all about?"

"It's about trying to make some money," I say.

"You do understand there are rules in the student guidebook about soliciting to the student body without approval from authorities," she says.

"I didn't know that, ma'am. I'm sorry. It won't happen again," I say again. I want to tell her everyone sells stuff to everyone around here. Candy, gum, homework, tests, smelly stickers, puffy stickers, cigarettes, matches, firecrackers, glue, pencils with those annoying pom-poms on the ends, all sorts of stupid junk behind her back, and here I am selling a service as beneficial and beautifying as braiding hair out in the open, and she puts an end to it.

"I will not tolerate my school turning into some black market," she says.

"No, ma'am," I say.

"I am well aware of the prohibited business transactions taking place on my school property, and I plan on putting an end to all of it," she says, and leans back in her chair. I stare down at my sorry duct-taped

Chucks. I hear her open a desk drawer. "Do you own one of these?"

I take a peek. Mrs. Farmer holds one of those pom-pom pencils. She wags it as she would a finger. *Naughty. Naughty. Naughty.* The orange pom-pom head bobs.

"No, ma'am," I say.

"Do you know who's been selling these silly things?" she says.

"No, ma'am," I say, looking her straight in the eyes. Avoiding eye contact is a sure sign of lying, so I make sure our eyes meet. I know who sells them, but I'm not telling. Her glasses, which are chained around her neck, hang off the tip of her nose. She takes them off and lets them hang against her chest like a bib. I look back down at my sad imitation Chucks. I need to get out of here. "Mrs. Farmer?" I ask.

"Yeeees," she says, leaning closer to me. She thinks I'm going to snitch.

"I'm sorry, but may I please go to the bathroom? I drank a lot today," I say, pressing my knees together.

She leans back and sighs in disappointment. "Very well, but no more of this," she says, tapping the pom-pom pencil on my flyers. "Consider this a warning. Next time I call your parents. Understand?"

"Yes, ma'am," I say, pressing my knees together and making the *I'm going to piss right here, right now* face.

"Close the door on your way out," she says.

"Thank you," I say, and leave.

With each step back to the classroom, my shame turns to anger. Call my parents. I dare you, Principal Farmer. My father is dead. My mother won't understand what you're talking about. I'll need to translate. I'll tell her you called to congratulate me on making Principal's List again and again and again. Straight As. *We are so proud of Ok. Ok is an excellent student. Ok will succeed in life.*

Call my parents. Good luck with that, Principal Farmer. Our phone might get turned off because we can't pay our bills. We're poor. You don't get it because you drive a shiny black Cadillac, and your family is all intact, like in the framed photograph in your own private office, where you control the lighting and summon model students like myself to torture them.

What did I ever do wrong? I've never gotten detention. I've never made trouble. I've never been called to your office. Who cares if kids are selling pom-pom pencils? What's wrong with that? It shows initiative and entrepreneurship. Why don't you leave us alone? Why don't you crack down on the bullies and the cheaters and the school-skippers and whoever's drawing swastikas on the bathroom walls?

My walk turns into a march. I feel so mad that my throat lumps up. I will not cry. No way. Did Clint Eastwood ever cry? I'm not going to cry because I got called to the principal's office. But I can't hold back the tears. A dam breaks. Tears gush out. My cheeks are wet. My nose runs. I drip all over the hall. I run to the bathroom, blow my nose, wash my face, and wipe myself dry. That's enough, crybaby. I fist up my porcupine hair and pull hard. I choke myself to get rid of the lump in my throat. I slap my cheeks. I pound my head against a stall. Stop it, crybaby. Stop it. A toilet flushes. I freeze. Walking out of a stall is Mickey McDonald. She sees me and says, "Oh my Lord, what on God's green earth are you doing in the girls' bathroom?"

"No! *You're* in the *boys'* bathroom," I say.

Mickey opens her arms, waving the hall pass along the bathroom walls like one of the models on *The Price Is Right*, and says, "See any piss pots?"

There are no urinals. Where have all the urinals gone?

"Knock, knock," Mickey says slowly, stepping toward me with eyes wide open.

I shake my head, backing into the mirror.

"This here's the part where you say, 'Who's there?'" she says.

"Who's there?" I ask.

"Urinal."

"Urinal who?"

"Urinal lot of trouble, perv," she says, bobbing her head like a rooster.

I run out of the girls' bathroom.

nine

Our class walks in a line to go to the library. I'm behind Cassandra Cruz. I lean in and tell her that her hair is a mess. It really isn't. It looks fine, but I'm trying to drum up business. Cassandra turns around and looks at me. Her eyes are big and round and dark, her lashes curling up to the ceiling. They remind me of eyes you find glued on dolls. I give her the *Sorry, but not my fault* look and shrug. As we walk, her hands keep touching her hair, trying to diagnose the mess and tidy it up. Her fingers pull, pat, and tuck loose strands. I lean in again and in my most matter-of-fact tone say, "You made it worse." The more Cassandra touches her hair, the messier it gets. And a girl like Cassandra cares a lot about how she looks.

"I can fix that," I say.

"In your dreams," she says, and yanks out three ponytail holders. Her hair looks like a tangle of chains.

"I can braid," I say.

"No, you can't," she says.

"Anyway, I wouldn't touch your hair," I say.

"Shut up," she says.

I keep quiet.

Cassandra turns around and asks, "Why not?"

I shrug.

When the class reaches the library, we all spread out, looking for books for our social studies reports. I find one about life in ancient Rome and hide in the back corner. I have a funny feeling Cassandra is going to come looking for me. Something about the way she told me to shut up was very promising. I sit on the floor, lean against the shelves, and open the book on my lap. I read about how the Romans stole most of their ideas from the Greeks. Those Romans were nothing but a bunch of bullies and copycats. I keep my nose buried in the book, as if I have important work to do, as if I don't want to be disturbed.

I wait. I hope. Please. Disturb me.

Then I hear rubber soles brushing against carpet. I keep my head down and turn a page. There's a drawing of Artemis, the goddess of hunting, with a bow and arrow ready to kill. Her arms and legs look strong. Her toga barely covers her breasts. Her long hair flows onto her face. I take a pencil, draw a bubble near her mouth, and write, "How am I to hunt under these conditions?

I can't see. Get this hair out of my face!" I draw a stick figure of me at her feet with a bubble that says, "I can braid it for you." Artemis points her bow and arrow down at me and says, "Do it. Now."

"Awww. I'm telling. You're writing in a library book," Cassandra says.

Without looking up, I turn the page and scribble some more. This feels wrong, but I have Cassandra's attention.

"I'm telling," she says.

"Suit yourself," I say, cheering myself on to play it mean.

I keep doodling. I draw stars, feathers, and dollar signs. I'm going to erase all this later. Cassandra stands there. The toes of her high-tops are scuffed with grass stains. She doesn't say anything. Drawing more dollar signs, I pray hard that she doesn't walk away and tell on me. The last thing I need is a second trip to Principal Farmer's office. Cassandra squats down and whispers, "Do my hair."

I try to play it cool like Clint Eastwood. I squint, tilt my head, shrug, make my best bored-to-death look, and begrudgingly say, "Fine."

Cassandra quickly sits down in front of me. I stand up. When she crisscross-applesauces her legs, her pants shrink, exposing her calves. They look gray, as if dusted with ashes, nothing close to the brown of her hands and face. I ask, "What happened to your legs?" She pulls her socks up as far as they can go and says she was in a really big car accident. While she talks on and on about this car accident that rendered her skin discolored, I place my hands on her head the way Pastor Chung lays his hands on the heads of the sick, praying for healing. Cassandra's hair is a tangle of curls, but it's soft like the stuff teddy bears are made of. I bet she doesn't even need a pillow for her head because her pillow is built in. Her hair feels so different from mine, which is all needles. I'm porcupine. She's poodle.

I take a small portion of hair and try to remember the pictures in the instruction manual. I divide my handful into three, cross the right piece, put it between the other two, cross the left piece, and put it between the other two. It's like a game. The third piece keeps breaking up the pair, and before it storms in to divide the two, it gathers up more hair or more forces from its side to conquer the alliance. Divide. Conquer. Reinforce. I'm doing it. I'm French-braiding Cassandra Cruz's hair. I can't get all the tangles out, but that's not a problem because they're holding the braid together. It forms down the center of her head, just like in the pictures.

While Cassandra goes on and on about how she almost died in that car accident, I say it. For the first time, I tell somebody. I don't know if I'm showing off and trying to one-up her tragedy, but I say, "That's nothing. My father fell off a roof, broke his neck, and died."

She pauses and says, "Oh my God. That's too bad." Then she continues about how her dad was in the same car accident but he didn't die or anything but there was blood everywhere and hundreds of ambulances and police cars and motorcycles showed up and—"Oh my God, you know *MacGyver*? Do you watch that show?"— the police officer wasn't really MacGyver but he looked just like him, and he carried her out of the car and told her to hold tight and she was going to be all right because he'd make sure of that and she was so lucky to be alive, but now she has to go to a dermatologist every week to get this special and very expensive medicine, which is, like, a hundred dollars, because if she doesn't use the medicine, her skin will fall right off.

Cassandra Cruz is all talk, but that's fine with me. I'm braiding her hair.

ten

Word spread fast.

Almost every girl in my class has some version of the French braid. The single braid, the double braid, the triple, the one-third, the one-side, the horizontal, the upside-down, the headband, the ring-around-the-entire-head. Demand is high. Girls follow me, stop me in the halls, pass me notes. This volume of attention from the opposite sex is unprecedented. I braid before school. I braid after school. I braid on the bus. I braid during recess. I braid during lunch.

With all this braiding, you'd think I'd be rolling in the dough by now, wearing Nikes, paying bills, moving out of the one-bedroom back into our two-bedroom apartment, getting rid of my mother's piles of sleeves and cuffs all over the floor. I can't move around our place without knocking them over.

Once, I had to run to the bathroom. I didn't mean to knock the pile over. Ŏmma yelled at me, called me a *pabo*, knuckled my head. She never used to yell at me. She never used to call me names. She never used to hit me. That was my father's job. He used to say under his breath, loud enough so I could hear, but soft enough so I felt guilty about eavesdropping, "When's this idiot going to be a human?" My father shoved me from behind to hurry me up, saying, "Why are you so slow? You move slower than an ant with all its legs cut off. Move, ant. Move." I wanted to turn around and push him back, telling him to stop pushing me and that slow and steady wins the race, but my mother would beat me to it and tell him to be quiet, look who was talking, look who took forever to get us into a house.

My mother used to stand up for me. She used to always make me feel better. If my father put me down, she cheered me up with a smile or a hug or a pat on the head or something yummy to eat. I never used to get goopy rice and soy sauce for dinner. Goopy rice is for the sick. I'm not sick. I'm a growing kid, and if I want to keep growing, we need more money.

I'm not making enough. These girls can't pay me fifteen dollars for each braiding session, as I'd priced in my business plan. They give me whatever they've got: a penny, a dime, a quarter if I'm lucky. All that work for $4.68. I need to hit it big, like win that talent show. Maybe I can braid onstage? I'd need to braid with my toes, dressed like a cheerleader, twirling batons and blowing "America the Beautiful" on the harmonica for any entertainment value.

My problem is that I'm having a really hard time saying no to these girls. They follow. They beg. They pass me notes. Please, please, please. Some of the girls come back the next day and say the braid didn't hold up overnight and this one part is loose, so can I do it again. So I do it for them because they're girls, and I can't say no to girls unless it's Mickey McDonald, and I like touching their hair and making them happy.

Some of them even hug me afterward. At first I thought they were coming in closer to smack me or something, so I ducked. But when they hugged me, and I felt their arms around me, my face would go hot and my hands would shake. A red face and shaking hands aren't good for business. But I got used to the hugs. You get enough of them, you kind of become immune. Adoration from your clients is part of the business.

I've also noticed that girls have a lot of secrets, and when you're doing their hair, all those secrets come spilling out. They start out by saying, "Don't tell anyone this, but . . ." Here are some of the secrets I've collected while braiding: Jaehnia is in love with Asa, and Asa is not at all interested in her in that way 'cause he's not into desperate girls and Jaehnia got desperation written all over her sad face. Monroe got the highest score on the math test, and that made Jack really mad and he started cussing at her in front of the whole class 'cause a girl beat him in math. Kym's parents are getting a divorce. It's not really a secret 'cause she's telling everyone about it. She must like the attention. Claudio got caught sneaking around under the back staircase looking up girls' skirts. What is wrong with boys these days? Why don't they got no manners? How come they be so nasty? "You are not nasty, Oak. You are different. I like you. I feel like I can tell you this, but promise me you won't tell anyone. Seriously, you cannot tell this to a single soul, 'cause if you do, oh my God, I'm going to be in so much trouble, but . . ."

I need to charge more for my services. I am both braiding booth and confession booth. I can't continue to conduct business this way. I'm not running a charity here. My fingers are getting tired. I've become the class gossip dump. I'm risking detention, suspension, and possible expulsion. My bright and promising educational future darkens. And for what? A fistful of dollars? On top of that, I don't even have time to eat lunch or go to the bathroom anymore. I need to charge one dollar per braid, and that's that. No if, ands, or buts. No buck? No luck. And then there's Mickey McDonald, who keeps eyeing me ever since the bathroom incident. I'm afraid she's going to say something and ruin my business. I now have more girls after me than Asa does—for different reasons—but quantitatively I am in higher demand, and I want to keep it that way. I dread the moment a client sits before me, my hands braiding her hair, and she says, "Oak, is it true you were crying in the girls' bathroom?"

eleven

On Saturdays my mother used to clean the apartment, do laundry, make banchan to last us the whole week, sew, sleep, watch TV, and make sure I had plenty to eat and did all my homework. We used to eat out on the weekends too. My father liked taking us to restaurants. His favorites were Ponderosa, Bob's Big Boy, and Beefsteak Charlie's. He insisted we order the steak dinner that came with a baked potato, green beans, and all-you-can-eat sweet rolls. He poured A.1. sauce over his steak. I liked mine with ketchup. My mother squirted hot sauce on hers. We finished the meal with slices of apple pie. We would walk out of the restaurant feeling stuffed, slow, and all-American. We don't do that anymore on Saturdays. Instead my mother works the cash register at Arirang Grocery from nine in the morning to seven in the evening, and I'm all by myself. It's all right. I kind of like it. I just hope she brings food home tonight. We're low on kimchi and rice.

We need another case of ramen. Our fridge is empty. There's nothing to eat.

I organize my money on the kitchen floor. All $11.68 in change. I stack my pennies, nickels, dimes, and quarters, entertaining possibilities. I could buy comic books, lottery tickets, a kite, a pizza, M&M'S, Kentucky Fried Chicken, "Finger lickin' good." I knock down my puny towers of change, thinking how far away $11.68 is from $100.

I could give the money to my mother. I miss her. I miss how she used to read the Korean newspaper to me after dinner and tell me Korean folktales that were supposed to teach me lessons, the main one being "Listen to your mother." I remember the story about the sandal peddler, who one day, while making straw sandals, began to laugh very loudly. He laughed and laughed and laughed. And then he died.

"So what's the moral of that story?" she asked.

"Laugh every day because it may be your last," I said.

"But didn't laughing kill him in the end?"

"No, because the day of his death was inevitable. It was good he had a joyful last day."

"Which is better? One day full of laughter ending with death, or one full of tears with more days to face?"

"More days," I said.

"Good answer," she said.

I could offer the money to God tomorrow, drop my coins onto the plate, make it go *chink-chink* like a soda machine swallowing quarters before making thirsty wishes come true. What blessings can $11.68 buy me?

I could save for a rainy day.

Rain isn't impossible today. There are plenty of clouds in the sky. It's windy, a good day for flying kites. Once, when my father was in one of his nostalgic moods, he and I flew kites that we had made with parchment paper and strips of bamboo. We smeared the string with Elmer's glue. We broke dead lightbulbs in a paper bag. We crushed the glass into powder and used it to coat the kite strings. We hung the glassed strings on the railings of our balcony to dry in the sun. My father told me, "You don't fly kites. You fight them." Once we got our kites in the sky, his attacked mine. I didn't want my kite to snap and crash. I didn't want his to snap and crash. Couldn't we just fly them for fun? I didn't want to fight, but my father kept at it, striking his string against mine until it snapped and my kite crashed. This made him laugh and laugh, just like a kid. It made me feel sore inside.

Today is rainy enough for me, so I put the coins in my pockets and a key around my neck, leave the apartment, and walk to Peoples. Our phone is dead, so my mother can't call to check on me. I have the day to myself. I'm free.

The automatic doors of Peoples open. I limp-strut in like I'm supposed to be here. If anyone asks, I'm picking up aspirin for my mom because she has a splitting headache. Better yet, she has her monthly period, and I was sent to buy maxi pads. That would shut them up and make them leave me alone.

I walk down the snack aisle. I don't want potato chips or Doritos or pretzels. Pass, pass, pass. What stops me is the Duchess glazed honey buns with the white icing suffocating under the plastic wrapping. They stand at attention in single file, as if saluting me. I take the one in the back. My mother taught me to always take from the back for the freshest selection. She should know. She works at a grocery store. The plastic crinkles its gratitude. I hold the bun gently in my hand, careful not to squeeze.

Last year for my birthday, my parents put a candle in the center of a Duchess honey bun, sang the happy birthday song in English, and watched me blow out one candle. This kind of shocked me because they never made a big deal out of birthdays. For Koreans, unless you are a one-hundred-day-old infant or a one-year-old or really, really old, birthdays just don't matter much. You don't get a party. You don't get cake and ice cream.

You don't get balloons. You don't get presents. You just get seaweed soup. It's what all the mothers eat to make breast milk. Seaweed soup accelerates milk production. In a way, this soup is your very first meal. And like it or not, it's going to be your birthday meal for the rest of your life. I like it just fine. The broth reminds me of creek water. The dark strips of seaweed flow like the hair of mermaids and slide down your throat like warm Jell-O. But what I don't like about it is that after having a bowl of this magical, milk-making potion, I always feel a little nervous that I might squirt milk.

With my Duchess in hand, I rush past the shoelaces and walk down the cosmetics aisle, where it's all about splash, spray, fresh, tingly, and ready for action. The sample bottles chant, *Try me! Try me!* I feel sorry for them. They look used and left behind, while the new bottles get picked by warm hands and taken home. *Try me, pretty please.* I'm sorry. Maybe later. No, thank you. I don't have money. I know it's free. Leave me alone. I'm here to get aspirin for my mom, who has a splitting headache.

I hurry to leave the aisle, when a bottle of Jergens lotion, with its teardrop shape, its TRY ME sticker smudged with fingerprints, its cap left open, and its spout crusted with dried lotion, speaks to me. *How can you walk away from me? Don't pretend you don't recognize me. You know me. You've seen me on your bathroom sink. Most recently, you saw me in the trash can. That's right. She's all out. She needs me. Haven't you noticed her hands lately? Drier than a dried-up squid. You deserved that knuckle to the head. The poor woman needs me, and you know it. You've seen her hands. Your mother's hardworking hands. You've cringed at their touch because they feel so . . . what's the word? Dry. By the way, where is she today? Oh, at work, working those dry hands to the bone, while you're here prancing up and down the aisles of Peoples with a honey bun. You should be ashamed of yourself.*

I have enough money, but I'm not going to spend it on lotion. I look up and down the aisle. The coast is clear. I take a bottle of Jergens off the shelf, tuck it into the back of my pants, fluff my shirt and jacket, and limp-strut to the registers. I pay for the honey bun, count my change, say thank you, and walk out through the automatic doors.

It's a good thing my pants are too small for me. The tight fit keeps the Jergens from sliding down my pant leg. The plastic bottle pressing against my skin makes my butt sweat, but I don't dare remove it. I hear police sirens in the distance. They're coming for me. I bet there are surveillance cameras at Peoples. They caught me on tape. They called the authorities. They're onto me. My heart rattles like a machine gun, forcing me to move faster. Run! Run for your life!

When I reach our parking lot, I slow down. The sirens are gone. All I can hear is my breathing. No one is around. As I walk by the Dumpster, I see a cat pacing near the side opening. It sees me and meows. I say, "What're you looking at, scaredy-cat?" and keep walking. As if wanting to pick a fight, the cat approaches me. It's gray with a patch of white on its nose. Its tail snakes like a whip in slow motion. The cat has only one eye. Where its other eye should be is a scabbed-up black hole. It meows, begging for help. I walk faster. It follows. I stop and tell it to scram. I bark. It meows, steps closer to me, and rubs its head against my ankle. "Please leave me alone," I say, and squat down to push it away. It feels warm and soft. I pet the cat, wishing the bottle in my pants were filled with milk. I open my honey bun, break a piece off, and hold it out to the cat. It sniffs and licks it off my fingers. "I'm sorry I can't help you," I say. It meows and walks away.

When I get home, I lock the door, pull down the shades, go to the bathroom, and grab the Jergens out of the back of my pants. I rinse the bottle off, dry it with a towel, and set it on the sink. I take a good look at myself in the mirror. I am a shoplifter. I stole. I shake my head, wanting to return to when I was three years old, my mother and father holding my hands and lifting me through a terminal on our way onto an airplane. "This is what flying will feel like," they said. "No reason to be scared. We're going to have so much fun," they said, and lifted me. I hung from their grips, suspended in trust and innocence, swinging my legs and laughing.

With all the shades down, our apartment looks gray, like a cloud hovers over it. I don't want to let any light in. I sit on the couch, listening. I hear familiar laughter coming from the TV downstairs. The refrigerator hums. A door in the hall squeaks open, squeaks shut. The hall echoes with footsteps. Our clock ticks. I listen for sirens. When I don't hear any, I open up the honey bun and bite into it. It's soft, sticky, and so sweet that my throat burns. I take another bite and another until the bag is empty. I lick the icing off the wrapping, crumple it, and throw it across the room. It lands next to one of my fake Chucks, which I threw off my feet in my rush to hide. The other one landed on the sewing machine.

I am bored. I stand on the couch, and because my mother isn't here to yell at me about throwing dust everywhere—but the dust isn't my fault, it's her fault, her sewing makes all this dust, and she isn't cleaning like she used to—because my mother never lets me, I jump on the couch. One, two, three cushions. The springs squeak in applause. The cushions pop out of place, bouncing in excitement. I can't reach the ceiling. I bounce harder. Each jump vaults me higher, higher, higher. My fingertips brush the ceiling. Maybe I can be an acrobat for the talent show. I plop down with the tired cushions, panting.

Light beams in along the sides of a window shade, yellow and wrinkled with age. The light is orange. It's sunset light. Dust floats in the air. My breathing slows. My eyes close. Thinking of smoke and my father's ashes, I fall asleep.

I dream that mermaids are waiting in line for me to braid their hair. We are at the bottom of the ocean, and I can't hold my breath long enough to finish a braid and keep the line moving. I keep coming up for air, and when I swim back down to finish my job, the braid has come undone, and I have to start all over again. The mermaids are very annoyed with me. I try to tell them that I'm doing my best, but I can't speak. My words come out in bubbles and gurgles. A light comes on. I open my eyes and see two blurry figures walk into the apartment. I close my eyes, pretending to sleep. The figures whisper.

"Deacon, can I get you something to eat?" my mother says.

(Like we have anything to eat?)

"No, please don't trouble yourself. It's been a long

and trying day for you. You should get some rest," a man says.

"Please, have a seat. These are Ok's things. I'm so sorry for the mess," she says.

(Not my mess. All this is your mess.)

"You should have a seat," he says, taking her arm and easing her down onto a chair.

(You don't have to touch her. She doesn't need your help to sit down.)

"We just moved, and I haven't had the chance to unpack everything," she says.

(What? Everything's unpacked. We unpacked everything.)

"Please don't apologize. I understand. You've suffered a great deal today. But we have much to be grateful for. You are alive. You have a warm and cozy home. You have a healthy son," he says.

"I worry about him, Deacon," she says.

(I make you worry? I cook ramen for you, I wash the dishes for you, I bring home As on my report cards for you. What trouble have I ever caused?)

"Do not worry. What does the Bible say? Worrying is a waste of your time and energy. It is a sign of your lack of faith. Obey our Lord and don't worry," he says.

"You're right. I'll try my best. It's just been very sad for me," she says.

(Stop it! You're making her cry.)

"Of course you're sad. It's a very sad thing to lose a husband. It's a very sad thing to lose a father. I should know. I've lost so much in my own life, two wives and a father at a young age. I was only ten years old, younger than your son," he says.

"I didn't know that," she says.

(Ewww, he's touching her arm. Get your hands off her!)

"But I wouldn't change any of my past. The suffering has made me the man I am today, although I truly believe that I would be a better man if my father had been there to guide me. Perhaps I would be more open, more trusting of others, more generous," he says.

"Oh, Deacon, you are very generous. And if you weren't open and trusting, you wouldn't have helped me today. I didn't know who else to call. I don't know what I would've done without you," she says.

(Why couldn't you call a taxi?)

"God was watching over you today. I am grateful for the opportunity to serve him by serving you. All things work for the good for those who have faith in God. If I can be more helpful, please let me know," he says.

(How about leaving already?)

"Thank you, Deacon," she says.

"Then I will leave you for now. Good night," he says.

(Finally.)

"Thank you again, Deacon. Good night. Go home safely," my mother says. She uses her church voice. I hate that voice, high and singsongy like a stupid three-year-old. She sounds fake. She doesn't sound like herself. She never used that voice with my father. She never uses that voice with me.

The door shuts. I open my eyes and rub them. The light stings. Once the room comes into focus, I see my mother sitting on her sewing chair. I feel queasy from picturing the deacon and her together. My mother's eyes are shut. Her hand covers her face. Her frizzy, home-permed hair looks like the brown of something burnt. The apron from Arirang Grocery hangs on her like a ghost of a baby. Her left leg is propped on a box. It's covered in a big white boot. My mother has a cast on her foot.

The only time I've ever seen a cast was back in second grade on Carry Morris. She was running home during kickball, fell, landed on her arm funny, and broke her wrist. She screamed and cried all the way to the school nurse's office. The next day her dad delivered her to our classroom soon after lunch. He kissed her good-bye, and she strutted in with a bag of McDonald's. I smelled the fries. Everyone flocked to Carry's desk to check out her cast and sign it. When my turn came, I noticed that her dad had written "OUCH" with a mustached smiley face in the *O*. Underneath he had signed, "Love, Dad." I was stunned that such a painful event could have such a happy ending.

I feel sorry. I want to go to my mother, put my hand on her shoulder, and tell her that story about Carry and her broken wrist, tell her that everything is going to be all right, but she looks so tired that I decide not to bother.

twelve

Pastor Chung orders the congregation to kneel and pray. I stop myself from nodding and smiling because my mother and I don't have to kneel, since her ankle is in a cast. But she grabs my arm to pull me down anyway.

"But your ankle," I say.

"What about it?" she says, turns around, and goes down.

She tugs at my shirt to bring me down with her. I don't want to because my jeans, tighter than ever, are on the verge of splitting at the knees and, worse, at the butt. But my mother pulls me down by my wrist, and the next thing I know, my head is where my butt used to be. She presses my face into the seat of the pew, and I'm getting a whiff of something that's making me think I could use a shower tonight. I put my hands in pray-position, discreetly using my thumbs to plug my nose. Those with the gift of speaking in tongues are pumping up their volume because, you know, God is deaf. My mother starts to do that rock-back-and-forth motion that makes me think of those ride-on ducks pooping out a coil of spring at the kiddie playground.

I close my eyes, exhale, and pray that I had nothing to do with my mother slipping on some ice that had spilled out of a tub full of mackerel. I was nowhere near the scene of the accident. I have an alibi. I was at Peoples buying a honey bun. And. And. I use my hands to face-mask my mouth and nose, and in one short breath I speed-whisper, "I-took-a-bottle-of-Jergens-for-Ŏmma's-dry-hands-without-paying-for-it." But what did that have to do with her falling and breaking her ankle and not being able to stand and walk and go to work and pay bills, buy food, buy me new sneakers? It's not my fault. God, you're the one to blame here. You're the one who's supposed to be watching over her. You could've gotten someone to clean up the ice or keep it in the tub with the fish, you're familiar with fish, you've worked with fish before, but no, you let her fall and you watched and you did nothing about it. Just because you saw me limp-strut out of Peoples with the Jergens doesn't mean you had the right to go and break my mother's ankle. Since you did it, why don't you undo it? Undo it. Now. In Jesus's name I pray. Amen.

thirteen

Before leaving for school, I bandage together three fingers on my left hand with white surgical tape and head for the bus stop.

On the bus a girl sitting in front of me turns her head and asks me to braid her hair when we get to school. I strategically scratch my ear with my bandaged hand and say, "Sure."

As she notices my injury, she looks sad and says, "Awww. But your hand is broke."

"Oh, this?" I say, and hide my hand under my book.

"If your hand is hurting, my braid can wait," she says.

"No, it's okay. I can still braid your hair. I need to keep working. I could use the money. I'm okay. It doesn't hurt that much," I say.

"What happened?"

"Umm. Sorry, but I don't want to talk about it. It's kind of embarrassing," I say slowly, stalling for time.

The girl turns her whole body around, kneels, leans over the back of the seat, and says, "Awww. It's okay. You can tell me. Promise I won't laugh. What happened?" Her sweet voice makes me feel like a cute puppy.

"There was this puppy," I blurt out as my cheeks heat up.

"Uh-huh," she sings.

"And it was black, and it had white spots, and it was very, very fluffy. And I was walking home from my bus stop, and I saw this little ball of fluff. It was bouncing around on the rocks near the creek. It was really cute. But then it fell into the creek. It was drowning. I wasn't even thinking. I just jumped in and scooped the puppy out of the water. I got all wet. So I guess I kind of saved the puppy's life," I say, nodding to cool down my hot head.

"Oh my God. That's, like, the bravest," she says. The girl sitting next to her has turned around, and some kids nearby listen along. Their heads bob in synchronicity as the bus stops-goes-stops, jerking us to school.

"So'd the dog bite your hand?" a kid asks.

"No, moron. You listening or what? He fell in the creek and crushed his hand on a rock," another kid says.

"Umm. Well. Not exactly. This is kind of the embarrassing part. Umm. There was this woman nearby. She was old. Really old. Her hair was all white. And she was probably blind, too. I'm not sure. Anyway, she was in a wheelchair, and she was screaming for help because it was her puppy that was drowning, so maybe she wasn't completely blind, but lucky thing that I was there and I saved her puppy. She called him Billy? I think? No, it was Barney. Yeah, because I remember thinking Barney like the purple dinosaur. Anyway, so I'm all wet and bring Barney back to her. I put him on her lap. She's trying to talk to me, but I can't make out what she's saying, so I have to kneel and put this hand on the ground for balance. She thanks me and starts rolling off in her wheelchair, but she rolls over my fingers because they're still on the ground. So that's how my fingers broke," I say, wondering how I might turn lying into a talent worthy of a stage, because I've sure captivated these kids. My story is getting eaten up.

The girl gets out of her seat, bends down, and hugs me. I feel her heart beat against my ear. She feels sorry for me. I don't like it when people feel sorry for me, but something about her sympathy makes my head dizzy and my whole body go limp and soft like a rag doll and my eyes water. I don't know why I feel like crying, but some knot inside of me starts to come undone. I try hard not to cry. She says, "Oak, you a hero."

Word gets around.

One girl makes me a get-well card. The "Get Well"

part is written out in a braid pattern. One girl draws me a picture of a princess with a long braid that flows down to her feet, with a puppy in her arms. Another girl gives me an apple-flavored Jolly Rancher. Another girl gives me a smiley sticker to put on my bandages.

The best part is they give me more money for braiding their hair. I think it's because they feel guilty about subjecting me to pain so they can have a good hair day.

"Can you braid today?"

"I don't know. My hand is still sore. The doctor says I shouldn't move it too much."

"Please? You did Lori's hair."

"That was yesterday. My hand was feeling better then. Besides, Lori gave me an extra dollar."

"I have an extra dollar."

"Fine, but only one braid."

"Thanks a lot, Oak. You're the best."

fourteen

Mickey McDonald, the girl with the roach-motel head of hair, corners me in the classroom closet. She hovers over me, stretching out her arms and spreading wide her orange-and-brown-zigzag poncho like a pair of wings. I think she's about to hug me, so I shut my eyes, stiffen my body, and wait to get it over with. Instead Old McD pushes me into the jackets hanging on the hooks, stares down at me with eyes as green as the Jolly Rancher melting in my mouth, presses her foot on top of mine so I can't run away, and says, "Braid my hair."

I look up at her hair. It's a mess. She has her own solar system, with her round pink face as the sun and the wads of tangles as planets orbiting her head in the shade Crayola calls Raw Sienna. The color reminds me of wet sand on a beach. I've been to the beach once with my mother and father. We built sand castles, jumped waves, and held our balance while Earth and ocean, as if in a tug-of-war, pushed and pulled. My father was a strong swimmer. My mother could hold her own in the water too. It was the first time I saw them playing together like two kids on a beach.

I show Mickey my bandaged fingers.

"Them fingers ain't broke," she says, grabs my hand, and squeezes.

"Owww," I say.

"Stop your bellyaching, you fraud," she says, bending my bandaged fingers into a fist.

I don't pull my hand away. I let her squeeze because I'm stunned. I'm ashamed. I'm scared. And I'm strangely relieved someone knows the truth. Mickey McDonald knows about me, and I have to admire her for that. How did she know?

"Here's the deal. You do my hair, and I keep my mouth shut. I keep my mouth shut about the little con you running here. I keep my mouth shut about finding you crying in the girls' bathroom. In exchange for my silence, you got to braid my hair for free," says Mickey. She talks like she belongs in a cowboy movie.

This is where Clint Eastwood would spit, but I skip the spit and just squint and say, "Fine."

fifteen

Mickey rides alone in the back of the school bus. She doesn't have friends. She's always alone. I guess I was too, before my braiding business took off, but she's more noticeably alone with that hair and those old clothes. She wants nothing to do with being invisible. I ride in the front of the bus.

We get off at our stop. I walk slowly so Mickey can follow. She follows me from a distance, playing it calm and cool. She looks like a spy. I cross the parking lot, pass the Dumpster, turn the corner of an apartment building backing up to the woods. As I wait against the brick wall, I peel off the tape around my fingers. It feels good to move them freely again.

Birds chirp. The yellow leaves of a maple tree glow in the sunlight. A breeze blows. Branches shake, and I think how it's nice that leaves fall while at their prettiest.

There are cigarette butts on the ground. I squat,

collect them into a pile, crush them with my fingers, and peel one open, uncovering the cottony filter and the leftover bits of ash and tobacco; this is something I used to do with the cigarette butts my father left in his ashtray. I smell my fingers and suddenly miss him. I suddenly feel like talking to him. Appa, my grades are excellent. My teachers all like me. I'm very popular in school now, especially among the girls, but I don't let the attention distract me from my studies and our plan for success in the USA. I grew an inch. I'm eating a lot of meat like you told me for the protein. I'm drinking a lot of milk like you told me for the calcium. I'm reading a lot too. I'm currently reading a book about the solar system and all the different planets. Did you know that the solar system formed about 4.6 billion years ago? Can you imagine that length of time? It's like eternity. Appa, is that where you are? Somewhere in eternity? Can you see from there? Can you hear from there? Can you feel proud of me from there?

Mickey's shoes appear before me. Startled, I quickly stand up, brushing ashes off my hands. Her sneakers look worse than mine. The rubber soles flap like loose tongues. We have the same holes on the tips, where our big toes bust out, except hers aren't covered in duct tape. She wears socks with pom-poms on the backs of the ankles. Mickey's pom-poms don't match. One is green; the other is yellow. And they don't look round and puffy the way pom-poms are supposed to look. They look mangled and chewed up like spitballs.

She hands me a comb. It's one of those small black combs the school gives out for free on picture day. It looks cruddy, and some teeth are missing. Mickey sits down. I stand over her pile of hair and go to work.

"Don't you brush your hair? How come it's so tangled?" I ask.

"'Cause I tease it," she says like I'm stupid.

"Why?"

"'Cause it needs body."

I'm not as gentle as I can be. I yank and pull, trying to run the comb through the knots. A lot of hair falls out. Mickey sheds.

"Owww," she says, and elbows my shin.

"Owww," I say, and knee her in the back.

She slaps my foot. I step on her other hand.

"You best watch yourself. My fingers are gonna get all broke up, just like yours," she says, and laughs.

"Hold still," I say.

Mickey sits still like a statue. She's unusually silent, and I wonder if she fell asleep, but she blurts out, "For your information, I know what a Medusa is. I looked it up. That was mean. I want you to take it back," she says.

"Fine," I say.

"Well, then I forgive you," she says.

"Okay," I say.

"And I take back 'ching-chong,'" she says.

"Fine," I say.

"Well, I'm glad we're all in the clear about that. You from China?"

"No."

"Then where you from?"

"You do realize there are almost fifty different countries in Asia?"

"So?"

"So, why does everyone think Chinese?"

"'Cause there are, like, a billion Chinese people. Higher chance of you being Chinese than, like, Mongolian. Do the math. So where you from?"

"Mars."

"So you're, like, a Martian?"

"I guess so."

"That explains a lot," she says, chuckling.

"I was born in Korea," I say.

"Where that at?"

"Next to China," I say.

"Everything's next to China," she says.

"Everything's made in China."

"I ain't."

"You don't say."

"Born and bred right here. I never lived outside Riverdale, Maryland, and I wouldn't have it no other way. Now, make it extra pretty," she says.

"Yes, sir."

"'Cause my daddy's visiting."

"Why does he have to visit? Doesn't he live with you?"

"My daddy's never lived with us. Ever. He can't stick around for more than two days," she says.

"Why not?"

"'Cause he drives a tractor trailer. He drives all over the country. That's his job. There ain't a state in the USA he ain't been to. He said the road own him. His wife and kids don't own him. That's for sure. I got a strong hunch he loves the road better than us," she says.

"Why?"

"'Cause him and my mom fight."

I get the knots out of Mickey's hair. It's easier than I thought. Her hair is oily, so the tangles come out easily. It feels smooth and soft. My fingers feel greasy, like they're covered in lotion. I comb gently.

"They fight like cats and dogs," she says, picking up a cigarette butt and squeezing out its insides. "I don't know why people say that, 'cause we got three cats and a dog, and they never fight."

"What kind of braid do you want?"

"Make it go around my head like a crown. You did it on that girl Crystal, and it looked so pretty. I couldn't stop staring at it. She looked just like a princess. I want it just like that. I want to look like a princess," she says.

"Okay," I say.

"Don't your parents fight?"

"No."

"Lucky duck."

"I guess."

"'Cause it's real ugly. I wouldn't wish that kind of hell on any child, not even the likes of Asa Banks. I hate that boy," she says, and squeezes the insides out of another cigarette butt.

"Yeah. Asa's a jerk," I say.

"I hate him. You know what he call me? He give me so many nicknames I can't even keep track. Old McD. White Trish-Trash. Mick the Hick. Mickey Gives Hickeys. You know what he said today? He was going around telling this one joke about me that went something like, 'Mickey McDonald look like Miss Piggy and a troll doll had a baby.' Only time he ever called me by my proper name. That one hurt. Makes you wonder, don't it? I mean, he takes all this time and effort to think up all these jokes and nicknames about me, for what? I don't know. Just makes you wonder, like, is he in love with me or something? 'Cause I seem to be on his mind a whole lot. I'm going to break his heart one of these days. I can't stand how he smiles. He smiles so evil. I swear he got Satan on his side," she says.

"Those troll dolls are cute, and Miss Piggy isn't bad. She's the best-looking Muppet," I say, and push her head down. I turn it sideways so I can take a small portion of hair from behind her ear. I divide it into three parts and start to braid.

"You trying to be my Kermit?" she says.

"Right," I say sarcastically.

"You can dream."

"You really bring out the amphibian in me."

Mickey laughs, taps my foot, and says, "Wait. Wait. I have a joke. What does a fat girl eat for dessert at Chinese restaurants?"

"What?"

"Four chin cookies."

"You managed to offend both of us in one joke," I say.

"So, you think I'm fat?"

"And you think I'm Chinese?"

"No, you're not Chinese."

"No, you're not fat."

"Shut up. Stop lying. I know I'm fat, and it don't bother me none. What bothers me is people's ignorance. Like no one's got a clue that way back when, being plump was the way to go. Plump meant healthy and attractive, and if you were bone skinny, no one wanted to marry you. That's why all those paintings from the Renaissance are full of plump women. It meant you got food, and you had money. And if you were skinny, it meant you were sick and poor," she says.

"Beauty is in the eye of the beholder. It's all relative. Take, for instance, tanning. Everyone here wants to get suntanned, but in Korea if you have a tan, people consider you a low-class rice paddy worker," I say.

"Well, I love laying out in the sun and getting me a golden tan," she says, running her fingers through clovers. Her nails are bitten down to stubs.

Mickey's neck is what Crayola calls Apricot. Her ear is covered in tiny hairs that make me think of newborn piglets.

"Look! It's a four-leaf clover!" she says, leaning forward to pick it.

"Hold still. You're messing me up."

"Today's my lucky day. Looks like you're not the only lucky duck around here. Hey, you doing the talent show? 'Cause I'm going to need you to do my hair for the show," she says.

"I don't have a talent," I say.

"Well, I'm going to be in it, and I'm going to knock their stupid socks off and show them all who's boss. I got stuff to prove, so I need you to do my hair. Hey, you should dress up like a Martian and braid everyone's hair."

"I'd have to braid with my toes to win," I say.

Mickey slaps her knee and laughs. I like her laugh. It's nothing like the fake, high-pitched laugh my mother delivers when Deacon Koh is trying to be funny. Or the laugh of ridicule that I hear at school. Mickey's laugh is real and sounds like it comes from someplace warm in her heart.

"So, aren't you going to ask me?" she says.

"Ask you what?"

"What my talent is?"

"Okay. What's your talent?"

"For me to know and you to find out," she says.

"Okay," I say, braiding past her neck. I'm almost up to her other ear. Her greasy hair is easy to work with. The oil acts like glue and holds the links together nice and tight. The rope pattern takes shape around her head. It looks like a crown. It looks a whole lot better than the tangled mess she had before. I wonder about what she said. What is it that she knows? What is it that I need to find out?

I finish. Mickey hands me a rubber band and bobby pins to tie and tuck in the tail end of the braid. She touches it, trying to get a feel for how her hair looks.

"How do I look?" she asks.

"Fine, but stop touching it. You're going to mess it up," I say.

"I am so excited I am going to piss in my pants. I need a mirror," she says, jumping up and down and moving her arms like a T. rex.

"If anyone asks, I charged five dollars," I say.

While she runs to the parking lot, I pick up my backpack and head home. I look over my shoulder and see Mickey admiring herself in the side-view mirror of a parked van. My hands feel oily. I check to see that no one is around and sniff my fingertips. They smell like puppies. I cross the field, kicking up leaves along the way. I look back to see if Mickey is still at the van. She walks across the parking lot toward the swimming pool. She walks with a bounce in her step, like someone who has something to look forward to. I pass the creek, wishing my father were driving in some tractor trailer on his way home to visit me.

sixteen

When I get home from braiding Mickey's hair, I find my mother on the kitchen floor, pounding cloves of garlic with a wooden mortar and pestle. She is surrounded by heads of cabbage, bags of dried red peppers, gingerroots that look like gnarled hands, a cutting board, a gleaming knife, onions, and a box of Morton salt advertising that when it rains, it pours.

My mother crushes the garlic, pounding it with a force that makes the ingredients tremble in fear. Without looking up at me, she says, "Where have you been? What have you been doing? Why are you home so late? Don't you care about your mother?"

"I'm sorry," I say, and put down my backpack.

As she continues to pound, she orders me to take care of the sewing. She says, "Get that stack of sleeves. Not that one. The one on the chair. Put it over there. Not there. Over there. Pack this other stack in that box. Not that box. The one next to the door. What's wrong with you? Can't you hear? Move. Move. Why are you so slow? Why are you moving like an old man?"

Her pounding and the garlic odor make me feel sick and hungry and hard of hearing. As I move a tower of sleeves to the couch, my mother yells, "Don't get that pile mixed up with the other one. Don't let it fall over. Don't leave it on the edge. Push it to the back."

I arrange everything the way she wants it. As she takes the knife and splits a head of cabbage in half, she says, "It's too dark over there. Put that lamp next to the sewing machine. I don't want you messing anything up. Sit down. Finish sewing those cuffs. Faster. Hurry. They're coming to pick up tonight. They're bringing money. After you finish that, I need you to go to the store. We have eleven kimchi orders. We have to make them tonight. Go to the store for me. Buy everything on that list next to the sewing machine. Don't forget a single ingredient. Take the bus. Take the shopping cart. Take the money in my purse."

As I sit at the sewing machine and turn it on, she says, "If we can't pay rent, we're going to be homeless. Do you want to be homeless and live under a bridge?"

"No," I say, threading the needle.

"If we can't pay rent, we'll end up in a stranger's basement. Do you want to live in a stranger's basement again?"

"No," I lie, and press the sewing pedal.

When my family first moved to America, we lived in a stranger's basement.

I was three years old. I remember the crickets, chirping and hopping across the floor, antennae moving like a pair of wands. I chased them, trying to cup one in my hands. They were too fast. My parents would tell me to leave them alone because they brought good luck. So I don't know why my mother threatens me: Do you want to live in a basement again? Because it wasn't bad back then. The three of us together.

I finish the sewing, pack the sleeves for pickup, go to the store, and bring back everything on my mother's list.

When I return, I find her asleep, sitting on the kitchen floor and resting against the refrigerator. The knee of her good leg is propped up, and the other in the cast sticks straight out, leaning against the basin of salted cabbage. Yellow rubber gloves cover her hands, the fingertips stained red. She wakes up, sees me, and slowly mutters, "Are you back already? That was fast. Come help me finish these orders."

I know how to make kimchi by heart. I've watched my mother. It's easy. You cut the cabbage and salt it. Wait a couple of hours. I do my homework during this time because I can't fall behind in school, otherwise I could end up making kimchi for a living for the rest of my life. Rinse the cabbage and drain it. Make the paste by mixing together garlic, ginger, onions, sugar, anchovy, red pepper paste, red pepper flakes, along with my mother's secret ingredient, which I can't divulge lest it ruin her kimchi business. Spread the paste all over the cabbage. Pack the cabbage in jars. Wait for it to ferment at room temperature. After a week the cabbage ripens, nice and sour. Refrigerate.

My mother tears off an inner leaf of the cabbage, tops it with paste, and shoves it in my mouth. The leaf is crunchy. The paste tastes fresh and strong. She looks at me, hovering over the basin, waiting for my approval. She asks, "Isn't it good?" I chew, giving her two thumbs-ups. She smiles.

We fill all eleven jars. My mother lines them up along the wall, lays her hands on them, and tells me to do the same. She prays, thanking God for her abilities, for our kitchen, and for me. She says I'm a good son and a good helper. She asks God to bless the kimchi, bless anyone who eats it, make the person strong and good and faithful. In Jesus's name. Amen.

We share a big bowl of rice with kimchi. We eat together, sitting on the kitchen floor. It's late at night. I'm tired. My hands tingle from touching garlic, onions, and peppers. My homework isn't finished. I have a science test tomorrow. But the rice is warm and soft in my mouth, and the kimchi is fresh, and my mother doesn't look sad and tired and worried, and she's not yelling at me or knuckling me on the head, and I can almost hear crickets chirping outside, making me feel like one lucky duck.

seventeen

s. Lincoln stands at the front of the classroom with a folder in hand. She says she wants some of us to read our essays entitled "I Am Grateful" before leaving for Thanksgiving break. The essays were written a week ago and displayed on the bulletin board. Out of curiosity, I read Asa's. He wrote about being grateful for the four Fs: family, freedom, future, and food. It was an impressive essay. Parts of it made me laugh and think that maybe he wasn't so rotten after all.

"Asa?" Ms. Lincoln calls.

His followers and some girls in the back cheer, saying, "Go, Asa!" He limp-struts to the front of the class, takes his essay from the teacher, clears his throat, looks down at his words, and begins to read. But what he's saying is completely different from what I read posted on the bulletin board. He keeps his eyes down on the paper and moves them left to right, just like he's reading. He takes pauses, pulls the paper close to his face, smiles, excuses himself for not being able to make out his own handwriting, and continues. Asa Banks makes up the whole thing as he goes along. He pretends to read, "I am grateful for the women in my life. My grand-mother, my aunts, my mother, my sisters, and all the beautiful young ladies of our sixth-grade class." The kids laugh. He goes on, "I am grateful the Pilgrims and Indians decided to put their differences aside and get along for this historic meal. It's an important lesson. Let's all get along for the sake of gobble-gobble." The class applauds. Asa hushes everyone down: "Shhh. I ain't done." He continues, "I am grateful it's almost Christmas, 'cause I was good this year. Can you say the same for yourself? I sure hope you can, 'cause Santa Claus is coming to town. Don't you frown. Don't you be a clown. Don't you be a hound. 'Cause Santa Claus is coming down to this here town." Asa crumples up his paper into a ball and throws it across the room into the trash can. He makes the basket, and the class stands up and cheers as if he scored the winning point.

"Asa! Charming, but would you please read what you've written—" Ms. Lincoln says, but the bell rings.

Everyone scrambles to leave. As I pack up, I'm puzzled and intrigued. Why didn't Asa read his essay? Was he embarrassed? There was nothing embarrassing about it. It was a good and humorous essay. Why didn't he show off as usual and read it out loud? Can't Asa Banks read?

As I walk out of the classroom, I pick up Asa's crumpled-up paper out of the trash and stuff it into my pocket, wondering who wrote it for him.

On the bus ride home I fantasize about what to do with my discovery. Blackmail. Extortion. Those Nikes would do just fine, probably three sizes too big, but I'll grow into them. I can't believe my luck. I know Asa Banks's deep, dark secret. He can't read and write. I chuckle, but I feel embarrassed for him. How did he make it to sixth grade? How did he get to be this old and not know how to read and write? He never read a book, not even a comic book? He can't read a cereal box. He can't make sense of a grocery list, street signs, and how so-and-so did it with so-and-so scribbled on the toilet stalls. He's never written anything, except maybe his name. Good thing it's short.

Asa has spent the whole year making my life miserable, but suddenly I feel sorry for him. He has no idea what he's missing out on. Or maybe he has an inkling but thinks it's too late to learn. My fantasies of blackmailing him turn to fantasies of teaching him how to read and write, which make me feel warm and generous inside, like I'm Jesus, Gandhi, and Martin Luther King Jr. all rolled up into one. This for sure would count as turning the other cheek. I fantasize about being best buds with him. We hang out, shoot some hoops, punch each other in the arm, but not too hard, and fart in front of each other and laugh about it. We laugh a lot. We laugh until our eyes water and our stomachs hurt and we piss in our pants. *Stop. Stop. You're killing me, Asa. You all right, Ok.*

eighteen

When I get home from school, I find my mother at the kitchen table, reading a letter. It's on tissue-thin par avion paper. Korean scribbles fill the sheets from top to bottom and side to side with no margins to spare. The letter looks like an ancient document holding secret messages. I walk into the kitchen to get a drink of water. My mother sighs, puts the letter down, and asks, "Ok-ah, do you want to move back to Korea?"

"I don't know. Do you?" I ask.

"No," she says.

"Then I don't want to either," I say.

My mother crumples up the letter, throws it into the trash, goes to her bedroom, and shuts the door.

I check our phone to see if we have service. She must've paid the bill, because the dial tone is back. I'm tempted to take the phone off the hook just in case Korea decides to call. The good part about having our phone service cut off was that we couldn't take calls from Korea. Soon after my father died, we got a lot of calls, most of them collect. They were very expensive. My mother couldn't deny the charges. I guess she couldn't say no to the mother of her dead husband, my grandmother. The early calls were sad. Then the calls got angry. She yelled at my mother, blaming her for her son's death. The later calls demanded money. My grandmother was convinced my mother had struck it rich from a life insurance policy. How else would she be paying for all her collect calls? Those calls made me feel relieved we were so far away.

My other grandparents were nicer about the whole thing. They didn't call collect. There was a lot of crying, but it was the sad kind of crying, not angry. They even asked for me. When I got on the phone, my grandmother asked if I remembered her. I said yes. Her voice sounded familiar like Ŏmma's, but deeper. She asked, "Don't you want to come home?" I said yes. When my grandfather got on the phone, he told me I was the man of the house now and to take care of my mother. I said yes. The calls ended with them telling us to come back to Korea, where we belonged, there was nothing for us in America, nothing but heartache and suffering and silence. I said yes.

My mother cries in the bedroom. I don't know what keeps her here. My grandparents want us to come back to Korea. She wouldn't have to work so hard. She wouldn't have to worry about ending up in a stranger's basement or homeless under a bridge. I'd get new clothes and shoes. We'd get plenty to eat. All our problems would disappear. Going back to Korea would be the easy thing to do. But just because something is easy doesn't mean it should be done. That was something Ms. Mason, my second-grade teacher, used to say.

I retrieve the letter from the trash, smooth it out, and try to decipher the message, but my Korean isn't good enough. Remembering Ms. Mason, I start folding the letter into an origami flower. She taught the class how to make a boat, a fox, and a frog with nothing but a sheet of paper. No scissors. No glue. No tape. It was like magic. Ms. Mason saw how much I got into it and taught me how to fold a flower. When I did the last steps of blowing into it and peeling down the petals, she said, "I know why you're so good at this. It's because you're so good at math. This is geometry in action."

Ms. Mason was my favorite teacher. She had a special saying for almost every occasion. "Get yourself to the bathroom before your eyeballs float." "If you've got the blues, dance it right off." "It's not about the getting, it's about the giving." She called nap time "playing possum." Imagine that. Those were her two favorite words: "imagine that." And she had a nickname for every kid in the class. She called me Okay. You know where that expression comes from? It was originally Greek, meaning "all good." Imagine that.

I put my ear against my mother's door. She isn't crying anymore. I don't know the whole story, but here's what I've pieced together: My grandparents didn't want their only child to marry my father because they believed he was a loser. Never finished high school. Spent too much time singing in bars. Too ambitious for his lowly talents and skills. No discipline. Thought too highly of himself. Smoked and drank too much. Lazy. And his ears had no lobes. No lobes meant no luck. When I was born, my grandparents came around to accepting the marriage. But then there was talk of moving to America. My grandparents didn't want us to leave the country. They forbade it. My father moved us anyway.

I think my mother feels embarrassed to go back. Returning to Korea means admitting she was wrong, that all the big decisions she made for her life and her family were bad ones. She failed. She has something to prove to herself and her family. She wants to be able to hold her head high. Returning a poor widow is not allowed. She'd rather end up hungry and homeless than give in to their *I told you so*. I respect that, and I don't.

I return to the kitchen to take the phone off the

hook. As I lift the receiver off, I hear ringing on the other end. My mother is making a phone call in her bedroom. The deacon's voice answers. Then my mother responds in her singsongy voice, "Hello? Am I calling too late?"

I hang up.

nineteen

eacon Koh picks my mother and me up in my father's Cougar to take us out to a Chinese restaurant for Thanksgiving dinner. A tree-shaped air freshener dangles on the rearview mirror, trying hard to mask any previous odors, but I can still smell my father's cigarettes.

There are times when I forget my father is gone. I don't know why, since almost every detail of my life has changed since we lost him. But sometimes when I'm sitting in class, or braiding hair while listening to a girl talk about her troubles, or just looking out the window, I have to remind myself that I don't have a father. Those moments don't last long. I wish I could forget right now because there are too many reminders here.

My father loved this car. He loved driving fast. He'd speed along George Washington Parkway, his favorite road, with me in the passenger seat. The windows would be rolled down all the way, our arms out, riding the beating wind like a pair of wings. My father would stick his head out and shout, *"Manse!"* I'd follow along and shout, *"Manse,"* which means "ten thousand years." You say it when you're having such an amazing moment that you want it to last for a long time.

A folded towel covers the driver's seat. As Koh helps my mother into the car, I lift a corner of the towel to see what's hiding underneath. A big fat copy of the Yellow Pages. Koh needs to sit on thousands of sheets of paper in order to fit into my father's sports car.

Wedged between the windshield and the dashboard is a black leather-bound Bible. There are no loose nails on the floor, no tar-covered work gloves, no cigarette butts and ashes in the ashtray. The Cougar has been cleaned out. The absence of these details makes me remember them more. And Koh has cleaned himself up for the occasion, wearing a light-blue dress shirt, a necktie, pants with razor-sharp creases, and polished brown leather shoes. I detect Old Spice. Even though he looks and smells church-approved, I don't trust him. I'd take my father's tar, cigarettes, and Johnnie Walker over Koh's pine-scented fake tree any old day.

Koh snaps on his seat belt and asks my mother to do the same. My father never wore his seat belt. He didn't believe in them. She pulls on the belt and looks for the buckle. Koh reaches over, dislodges it from the seat, and holds it steady while my mother locks in the tongue. *Click.* Just like the sound of the dead bolt on our door to keep thieves from breaking and entering. Is Deacon Koh a crook? Is he scheming to steal my mother away?

Their hands touch.

"Deacon, you're very careful," she says.

"Of course. I have to be when I have passengers who are VIP. Do you know what 'VIP' stands for?" he asks, raising his voice and looking at me in the rearview mirror.

I want to tell him boo-ee is not a letter in the English alphabet. *V* is pronounced vee, not boo-ee. To make the *V* sound, don't make kissy lips. Instead bite down on your lower lip. Vee.

"No," I lie, and look out the window.

"No problemo. I'll tell you. It's 'very important people,'" he says slowly.

What a jackass. His short tongue is trying too hard to sound American, and "very important people" comes out as "belly impotent peeper." By the way, "VIP" stands for "very important person," not "peeper."

"It actually stands for 'very important person,' but since there are you and your son here, I changed 'person' to 'people.' 'Person' is used for one. 'People' is used for more than one," he instructs, and chuckles, so very pleased with himself. "Am I right, Ok?" he asks, looking for me in the rearview mirror.

"What?" I say, trying not to vomit.

"I was just teaching your mother here some English. Your mother told me English is your best subject at school. She said you enjoy reading and writing. That's very good. They're important skills. But do you know what subject is more important?" he asks, clicking on the turn signal.

"Math," I say, hoping to shut him up.

But he keeps talking about how math is the foundation to all progress in civilization, how it's the language of logic, how he has a math degree, how math is what builds bridges, sends rockets to space, gives us clean water, blah, blah, blah. He says, "God is in math. Oh sure. The concept of infinity. That is God."

This equation comes to mind: Appa > Koh.

I stare out the window. We drive past my father's dream house. It's a big old abandoned house with boarded-up windows, a collapsing porch, a chimney big enough to fit Santa, and ivy shrouding its walls. It looks haunted. It's condemned and ought to be bulldozed, I heard. My father wanted it. We walked by that house many times. My mother thought he was crazy and never came along. Once, we even walked around it, making our way through the tall weeds as my father inspected its structure. He said it was a strong house with a solid foundation, they didn't make houses like this anymore, it was worth investing in, could very well be the ticket to his success in the USA. He wanted to buy it, fix it up, live in it, then sell it. He'd start with the roof.

We are getting on the highway. As gears shift, the Cougar jerks and picks up speed. The engine sounds the same, like the growl of a big cat. I look out the window. With most of the leaves gone from the trees, I can see the orange sky through the mesh of branches. The sun is setting. Cars pass. People are on their way to Thanksgiving dinners. Last Sunday at church Pastor Chung preached that if we felt sad, we should count our blessings. Make a list of all the things we were grateful for. Not focus on what was lost. Focus on what was found. I'm grateful for trees and how their roots keep the earth from crumbling apart. I'm grateful leaves grow back every spring and that they burn bright with colorful splendor right before they fall. I'm grateful for the sky, how it goes on forever, defying time and space. I'm grateful my mother's ankle is healing. I'm grateful for Mickey's laugh. I'm grateful I can ride in my father's car again. I'm grateful that even though I sometimes try to forget, I still remember him. My wish to forget only means I miss him.

I remember how my father used to say his most favorite parts of the fish were the head and tail, and he'd devour them enthusiastically, leaving the middle portion for me and Ŏmma. I used to believe the head and tail were his favorite parts, but looking back now, I wonder. I wonder if he was just pretending to like them so we didn't feel so badly about getting the best part.

I remember how he'd sit in a circle with his friends and play *hwat'u*, a Korean card game, among cans of beer and cigarettes. Once, he let me sit on his lap. He let me throw down a card. He let me take a sip of his beer. When I grimaced at the taste, he laughed.

I remember when my father and I were at a bank together, making a deposit. The bank teller was dressed in a shirt and tie and wore a plastic name tag. His name was Charles. He had on a gold watch. His fingernails were clean. I asked my father if he'd be proud of me if I became a bank teller, and he looked down at me and said, "I'm already proud of you."

I remember the weight of his hand on my back, as he patted me for doing something right, like translating a letter from the bank for him or making a phone call inquiring about a credit card application for him or writing a letter to the landlord about a window that wouldn't open because it had been painted shut by the previous tenants. He'd smile and pat my back, his pride and gratitude in my abilities superseding any embarrassment about his own limitations.

I remember how he sang Korean love songs and how my mother would join in. When she forgot the lyrics, he'd feed them to her, and the two of them would finish the song together.

I remember how he used to tell me this one Korean folktale about the disobedient frog, and how he made his mother suffer so much by his naughty ways that she died and ended up being buried near a stream, so the frog sat nearby and guarded her, croaking his sadness and regret. And my father would end the story complaining about Koreans and our unhealthy attachment to suffering. He'd ask, "Why can't the frog and his mother live happily ever after?"

When the food arrives, Koh bows his head, closes his eyes, and prays, "Heavenly Father, we thank you for this day. We thank you for the nourishing food you've placed before us. May we grow in faith and love for you, especially young Ok. May he grow in your strength and grace. May we become like a family, true children of God. In Jesus's name we pray. Amen."

I open my eyes, wondering why the man couldn't have said grace before the food arrived, before the smell of shrimp fried rice could taunt and torture me. I'm starving. My mouth waters. I want to scoop chunks of sweet-and-sour pork into my mouth. I wait for my mother to be served first. Koh handles the platter of sweet-and-sour pork like he's in slow motion. I finally get some on my plate and take a bite, and instantly all is well. I don't even mind that Koh stuffs his cheeks like a squirrel and that my mother daintily picks at her food like she's the queen of England when I know she wants to dig in like a peasant. I'm grateful for sweet-and-sour pork. I'm grateful for the big, noisy Chinese family at the table in the corner; otherwise, it would be more English lessons with Koh.

"Ah, Ok has a good appetite," Koh says.

"Slow down," my mother says.

"The secret to good digestion is thoroughly chewing your food," he says.

I spoon rice into my mouth and swallow.

"How does your school go?" Koh asks in English.

"Fine," I say.

"Nobody bother you?" he asks.

"No," I say.

"Nobody bother me, either," he says, and winks like Jhoon Rhee's son in the tae kwon do commercial.

I stuff my mouth with more rice and swallow. As I keep food in my mouth, because it would be rude to talk with my mouth full, I wonder if I can do some kind of martial arts demonstration for the talent show. I've watched enough Bruce Lee to know how the moves go. Kick, punch, make some karate sounds, do some cartwheels, break a board. It's all about putting on a show. The school probably already thinks I'm a black belt anyway, since I'm "Oriental," and all "Orientals" train in martial arts. I don't want to play into the stereotype. Maybe I'll polka instead.

The check arrives. I take a peek at the total and wonder how many heads of hair I'd need to braid to afford such a meal. A lot. Along with the check, there are three fortune cookies, which remind me of Mickey's joke. My mother places one cookie in front of each of us. As Koh pulls out his bulging black wallet full of cash and cards, I break the cookie. I nearly scoff out loud when I read my fortune. "You are among the best of friends," it says.

Koh places three twenties on the little plastic tray and thumbs through the wallet as if counting his bills. He pulls out a photograph and gazes upon it fondly. He shows my mother the photograph. She politely smiles, nods, and says, "How very intelligent looking." He shows me the photo, which turns out to be of a dog with long, floppy brown ears and a white wishbone of fur running down the middle of his face. This is his dog. Deacon Koh has a dog. I can't believe he has a dog. I want a dog. He's a beagle named Lassie.

I burst out laughing.

Koh drives us home. He walks my mother and me to our apartment building.

"Thank you," he says to her.

"Thank you," she says to him, and elbows me to say thank you.

"Thank you," I say, feeling exhausted from being thankful all evening.

"Let me help you," he says, reaching for the doggie bag in my mother's hand.

"It's fine," she says.

"Are you sure?" he says.

"We'll see you on Sunday," she says.

"Until Sunday," he says.

"Drive carefully," she says.

"Good night," he says.

It's all very horrible and tiring and boring to stand here listening to this nonsense. I open the door and enter our building. My mother steps in behind me, while Koh says, "Happy Thanksgiving."

"Happy Thanksgiving," she says.

The door finally closes. My mother sighs. I take the doggie bag as she takes my arm and limps up the stairs. When I get into the apartment, I hurry to the window to make sure Koh isn't hanging around under our balcony like some lovesick Romeo. His lonely figure moves swiftly through the shadows. The headlights come on.

He drives to the stop sign. He stops. The right-turn signal blinks. He's a careful driver. My father never would've come to a complete stop on a holiday night with no one in sight, and he wouldn't have bothered signaling. At least the Cougar is safe. Koh turns right and drives out of the parking lot, prowling away into the night.

twenty

The next morning my mother asks me, "Do you think the deacon is good-looking?" Then she answers her own question. "He's not exactly good-looking, but he's not bad-looking either. Looks aren't important anyway. What's most important is if he's kind. Do you think he's kind?" Before I can respond, "No, not really," she answers, "I think he's nice. Did you see how he made sure I put on my seat belt? He paid for dinner. He walked us home, too. That's a real gentleman. He has a house and two cars. He's a businessman. They make a lot of money. Don't you want to live in a big house? You would have your own bathroom. Don't you want your own bathroom?"

"Sure," I say, shrugging.

"Bathrooms aren't that important. What I really want for you is to have a role model to follow. Deacon Koh is a good example for you. He's different from everyone we know. He doesn't work long hours running a store. He doesn't labor with his hands. He uses his mind to make a living. He works smart. He knows things. He's sophisticated. He can teach you. I want you to learn all you can from him. He knows a great deal about making money and buying real estate and business opportunities," she says.

"I heard he made money off dead people," I say.

"Where did you hear that?" she asks.

"Church."

"Who said that?"

"Some *ajumma*s in the kitchen."

"What exactly did they say?"

"I don't know. They said something about the deacon getting rich after his wives died, because of some life insurance or something like that," I say.

My mother covers her mouth. She looks horrified. She says, "Those gossips! They work like dogs to make a living, and they see someone doing it without having to run a store or cook and clean for other people, and it makes them feel worthless and stupid, so they spread nasty rumors. If we'd known to get life insurance, we wouldn't have it so hard right now. We wouldn't be living like this. Deacon Koh's been talking to me about preparing for the unexpected. He said that a life insurance policy for me is very affordable, since I'm still fairly young and healthy and a woman. It's cheaper for women. And policies for children are even less. He said to see it as an investment. The money will grow in value over the years. It can help pay for your education," she says.

"Fine," I say.

"The deacon is a very smart man. He knows a lot about money. He doesn't live from hand to mouth like the rest of us. Ok-ah, there are two kinds of people in this world. People who labor with their backs and people who labor using their minds. I want you to be one who uses his mind. It's too late for me, but you can do it, especially with someone like Deacon Koh around," she says.

"Why is it too late for you?" I ask.

The question makes my mother stop.

"Like you said, you're young and healthy, and the insurance companies see value in that, so why is it too late for you?" I ask again.

"It's too late. It's too late for me," she says, her eyes tearing up.

"I'll do it. I'll do it. I'll learn everything from Deacon Koh," I say quickly, because I don't want her to cry.

"Do you promise?"

"Yes, Ŏmma. I'll do my best. I'll learn as much as I can. May I go outside now?" I ask.

"*Aigo, aigo*, you're such a good son. Be careful," she says, patting my head.

I put on my shoes and coat, hurry out the door, and run toward the parking lot, making an escape from my mother's latest ambitions for me to become like Deacon Koh.

Not many cars around. Some boys make free throws at the court. I run to the swimming pool, hold the fence, and catch my breath, looking into the bottom of the empty pool and remembering my father telling me there are two kinds of people in this world: those who swim and those who drown. I'm drowning in stress and pressure. My father was supposed to show me how to swim. Who will teach me now?

Someone covers my eyes from behind and says, "Guess who?"

I immediately recognize the voice, and the cold fingertips feel good pressed against my eyes. "Oh, it's you," I say.

"Say my name or I ain't letting go," she says, and laughs.

"Mick the Hick?" I say.

"Shut up," she says, lets her hands go, and slaps my back. "How'd you know? That's so mean. I hate that. It's not even original. It's just stupid. How'd you like it if I called you Uk?"

"I don't care. Everyone butchers it anyway. Join the club," I say.

"How you supposed to say it? Ain't it like 'oak'?"

"Actually, it's Ok," I say.

"Oak."

"Close enough."

"No, it ain't. Tell me how to say it."

"Say 'pork.'"

"Pork."

"Drop the *p* sound."

"Ork."

"Drop the *r* sound."

"Ok."

"That's it!"

"Ok. Ok. Oh, I get it."

"Don't move your lips when you say it. They have to hold that O shape the whole time."

"Ok. Oak. Hey, you're right," she says.

"Yeah, the position of your lips and tongue determines what sound comes out of your mouth," I say.

"You oughta be a speech doctor."

Mickey stands taller than usual. She wears a shaggy green coat made of fake fur that's clumped and matted like old carpet. On her feet are a pair of roller skates.

"Why do you dress like that?" I ask.

"'Cause it's retro. It's my style. You wouldn't

understand," she says, throwing on the hood and twirling around like a model. There's a tear in the back of the coat.

"That's not retro. That's just old," I say.

"Look who's talking, Mr. Ratty Old Jeans are so tight and tore up, why you even bother to put them on?" she says.

"I guess because I don't have anything else," I say.

"You lie," she says.

"Fine," I say.

"You just trying to tug at my heartstrings and make me feel sorry for you," she says.

"Okay," I say.

"No, for honest to God, you ain't got no other pants?" she says.

"Not really. These are it," I say.

"Oh my Lordy, I am so sorry," she says.

"Why? It's not your fault." I lean against the fence.

Mickey's hair is still in the braid I did days ago, sort of. Strands of hair stick out all over her head as if in constant static. She looks friendly and cheerful. She looks like she can give satisfying hugs. I know hugs, since I've received my share due to my braiding business, and not all hugs are created equal.

"How'd you know I was here?"

"Spied you at my window. See? I live right there.

That's my room. I was just looking out the window, bored to death, when there you were, running for your life," she says, balancing on her skates. They're white with red and blue stripes.

"You can skate?"

"No, Einstein. That's why I have them on, 'cause I like falling flat on my face."

I tap her shoulder, say, "Tag, you're it," and run because there's a part of me that wants to see Mickey McDonald fall flat on her face. There's also a part of me that wants to see if she can really roller-skate. I bolt for the creek.

"Grrrrrrrr," she growls, pretending she's a bear. She comes after me.

Mickey McDonald might not be much of a runner, but the girl can skate. Fast. On concrete, asphalt, grass, and gravel. I can't lose her. I make a sharp turn around a building. She follows. I hide behind a car. She finds me. I lose steam. I need to catch my breath. I jump into the creek and hide in the tunnel, which makes things worse because it amplifies my panting like an echo chamber.

"I hear you," she says, and climbs down the rocks, tiptoeing on her stoppers. She rolls into the tunnel and says, "Yoo-hoo! I see you!" Her voice echoes. I run toward the other end, where the opening is the size of a doughnut.

Halfway through the tunnel I look back and Mickey is gone. Probably too scared of the dark, too chicken to get her precious skates wet. My feet, shoes, and pant legs are soaked. I feel cold. I slow down and jog, checking out the graffiti. I walk past a plump black heart pierced with an arrow, blood dripping off its tip.

I reach the other side. Sitting on the trunk of a fallen tree, Mickey waits for me. Her cheeks are flushed pink. Her breath appears like fog in the cold air. "What took so long?" she asks.

"I stopped for a smoke," I say, crawling out.

Mickey laughs loud and hard. She leans back and fills the air with her guffaw. She isn't laughing at me. She's laughing at something funny I said. There's a difference. This laughter doesn't make me feel small or turn my face hot and red. This laughter makes me feel big and happy. I want to say something funnier to keep her laughing, but instead I walk past her.

"Hey, where you going?" she says.

"Home," I say.

"Oh no you're not," she says, and stands up, blocking my way. She tousles my hair. I pull away. She tries to create a side part and pat down my bristles, which keep springing back up.

"It's not like I need a comb-over," I say.

She laughs again. I like her laugh. She taps my shoulder and says, "Tag, you're it."

"I'm going home," I say.

"No fair," she says.

"I'm wet. I'm hungry," I say.

"We got leftovers, and you can borrow one of my dresses. Hey, I got an idea! How about you comb over to my place?" she says.

Her invitation stops me. Not only does her corny play on words make my insides flip with lightness and delight, but never in my life have I been invited to the home of another schoolmate. Never. Not one birthday party or sleepover. Not one want-to-come-over-after-school sort of deal. Mickey McDonald isn't my first choice, but I'm curious. I also don't want to go home wet and listen to my mother talk about her new boyfriend. I'm also hungry.

"Okay," I say.

"What's your favorite part of the turkey?"

"I don't know," I say.

"I hope it ain't the legs, 'cause they're gone. I got one, and Benny got one. He sucked on that bone like it was a pacifier. The boy is seven years old. That's just shameful. A seven-year-old ain't suppose to suck on a pacifier. So I knocked it out of his hand, and he cried like a big old baby. Then Charlie got a hold of it off the floor. Charlie's our dog. Benny chased Charlie down. They was tug-of-warring for the bone. Benny won, and then he stuck it right back into his mouth and sucked. Didn't even clean off the dog cooties. Gross. You know dogs eat poo and throw up, right? You got any pets?" she asks, spinning on her skates.

"No," I say.

"Well, we got three cats and one dog. Charlie, Sabrina, Jill, and Kelly. Get it?" she asks, balancing on one skate.

"No," I say, wondering how she isn't falling. If I could spin like that, I'd skate for the talent show.

"You don't get it? Charlie, Sabrina, Jill, and Kelly? Oh man! It's Charlie's Angels," she says, and stops skating to look at me like I'm completely out of it.

"Oh, like that old show," I say.

"I loooooove Charlie's Angels. They don't make 'em like that anymore. I can get my hair to look like Jill's if I tease it up real big. Kelly is a boy cat. But that's okay. He don't know no different. It's like when Benny was little, and I put makeup on him and dressed him up like a girl and made him do the Miss America walk," she says, and pretends to be Miss America, holding a bouquet in one arm while the other is raised in the air, her cupped hand oscillating like a periscope. She adjusts her crown so it doesn't fall off. She smiles big, waves, brushes away tears, mouths, "Thank you, I love you," and blows kisses at the audience. She's good, like she's done it a million times, which makes me wonder if this is her talent for the show.

She makes fun of Miss America, while wanting to be Miss America at the same time. I know that feeling. Mocking the impossible happens when you know something you want badly is out of your reach and you give up trying and make fun of it instead so you don't feel so lousy.

Mickey is funny, and she's smart. I smile, but I keep myself from laughing and applauding because she's the friendless Old McDonald of the class. I don't know why no one likes her. Then she turns her backside to the adoring audience, sticks out her butt, and lets one rip. Loud. Like the final call of a sick and dying bassoon. I laugh. She laughs. Her pink gums show. She snorts and shakes. I hold my stomach and laugh out loud until my eyes fill with tears and my stomach cramps and my cheeks feel warm and I want to make Mickey McDonald my best friend.

"Mick!" a voice calls.

Mickey stops laughing and looks up. A woman stands on top of the hill. She wears an orange jacket over a long yellow bathrobe. Her hair is yellow too. She looks like the setting sun. She inhales on her cigarette, blows out a stream of smoke, and taps off the ashes into the grass. Once she sees that Mickey is walking toward her, the woman turns and leaves.

"I gotta go," Mickey says over her shoulder, and takes off.

Her green shaggy coat hangs off her shoulders. Her pants hang low, showing a patch of pale skin. She hitches up her pants as she skates to the woman, who is already out of sight. That must be her mother, the one who cooks their Thanksgiving dinner. What's my favorite part of the turkey? I like the leg too. I like holding the drumstick in my hand and biting into the meat like a Viking. What's my favorite side dish? My first favorite is the stuffing. My second favorite is sweet potatoes with marshmallows. What's my favorite dessert? Even though pumpkin pie is the more traditional Thanksgiving dessert, I'm going to say apple pie because I've never tried pumpkin pie in my life.

twenty-one

During science class Mickey walks by and puts a note on my desk. The piece of paper is folded into a football. It has "PORK" written in capital letters with the *P* and *R* crossed out. I stare at it.

That's pretty clever. I want to stand it on its tip and flick it across the room for a field goal, but that means touching it, and I don't want to touch it.

Then Asa walks by, takes the note, and slips it into his pocket. He limp-struts to the pencil sharpener and takes his sweet time sharpening his pencil. When he's done, he holds it between his teeth and limp-struts back to his desk. As he passes me, I say, "Give it back."

"Make me," he says, biting down on his pencil.

"No one can make you do anything, Asa. I'm asking nicely to please give it back," I say.

"And I'm asking you nice to go make me an egg roll," he says, laughing so loud that the pencil falls out of his mouth.

I evil-eye him, struggling to breathe.

"Boy going to stare me down? How you see through them slits?" Asa says.

"I can see just fine. I can read just fine too. Can you? Can you read, Asa?" I say.

"Shut up."

"What're you going to do with a note, anyway? You can't even read it. You're illiterate," I say.

Asa bucks, knocking over the book on my desk, and stares down at me. I stare back. I'm very familiar with the look of worry in someone's eyes, and Asa looks worried. He throws the note at me and walks away. Now I understand the true meaning of the saying "Knowledge is power." I feel powerful. I beat Asa.

I hold the note in my desk, feeling 80 percent dread, 19 percent curiosity, and 1 percent excitement. The excitement is probably left over from having beaten Asa. I unfold the note, wondering what nonsensical message Mick has. *I like-like you. Do you like-like me? Check yes or no.* My heart pounds as I look down to read it.

It's a drawing of two stick figures running. The smaller stick figure, with the big, round head and needles for hair and shoes that have holes and drip water, is being chased by a stick figure with a big, round body and wheels on her feet and a Miss America crown atop troll-doll hair and a turkey leg in one hand and puffs of gas coming out of her butt.

It's funny. Mickey's cartoon makes me laugh. I don't like-like her. No way. But she's all right.

I fold up the note and put it in my pocket.

twenty-two

After church service Deacon Koh takes my mother and me out to lunch again. He has taken us out the last two Sundays. He took us to Pizza Hut the first time. Then he took us to Kentucky Fried Chicken. Today he's taking us to McDonald's. The whole world seems to be eating at McDonald's after church. It's packed with people dressed in their Sunday best. Even the McDonald's workers wear hats, green-and-red elf caps like Santa's little helpers.

There are no empty tables large enough for the three of us, so my mother and Koh sit at a table for two, while I sit behind them at another table for two. This is perfect. I wish we could always sit like this whenever Koh wants to take us out on a date.

I bite into my Big Mac. I get my book out and read *My Side of the Mountain*, which Ms. Lincoln strongly recommended. Like me, Sam hates his life. Unlike me, he does something about it. He leaves his family in the city and runs away to the mountains. He ends up living in a hollow tree. He befriends a falcon and a weasel. He eats plants and animals to survive. He wears deerskin. I admire Sam. I wish I could be like him. Get up and go.

A man puts a tray down across from mine and asks, "This seat taken?"

My mouth is full, so I shake my head no.

"Mom, come sit here," he says, and helps an old granny into the seat. He leaves her with me, while he goes to sit in a booth near the bathrooms with his wife and three kids.

The granny sits hunched over. Her hands tremble as she unwraps the cheeseburger and brings it to her mouth. Her head trembles too. All the trembling makes it very difficult for her to eat. She's never going to get the sandwich in her mouth, but she finally does and chews with her lips pressed tightly together. The red lipstick bleeds into her deep wrinkles. Her hat looks like a blue puddle about to slide off her head of thin white hair. She must be a hundred years old.

Behind me, Koh talks about the apocalypse. Bible says this. Bible says that. My mother tells Koh she wants to take English classes. Koh says it's important to prepare for the future because one never knows what the future holds. Hope for the best. Prepare for the worst. Has she thought more about getting life insurance? My mother says she wants to learn to drive. Koh says he wants to visit Hawaii. Hawaii is just like paradise and wouldn't it be wonderful to see it together, just him and her?

"Deacon. Please," she whispers loudly.

I feel her eye the back of my head. I know she mouths to Koh to be quiet so they don't make me feel like the third wheel. Three's a crowd. I suspect they resort to passing notes to each other or communicating with sign language so I can't eavesdrop on their plans for dumping me and starting a new life together, just the two of them. Aloha-ha-ha.

I feel sick to my stomach. I want to get out of here. I take a sip of my Coke. I prop up my book. As I turn a page, I see the granny's shaking hand reach toward me. Wrinkly, bony, covered in spots and veins, her hand, curled like the talons of a falcon, creeps closer and closer. I pull back, shielding my mouth and neck with the book. Is she trying to cast a curse on me? Is she trying to choke me? I nearly jump out of my seat when her hand stops over my tray. Her trembling fingers pick up a fry, dip it in my blob of ketchup, and aim it at the moving target: her mouth opened wide. She is stealing my fries right before my very eyes, but I want to cheer her on. *Come on, you can do it! Get it in! There! You did it!* She gets the fry into her mouth. While chewing and swallowing, she reaches for another. The granny is eating my fries.

I pour the rest onto her tray. As the fries spread out before her, the granny giggles like a girl and says, "Hot diggity!" Pointing her crooked finger at me, she slowly declares in her quivering voice, "You are a real man."

I realize she's a stranger. She's old. She probably has blurry vision. Her hearing is going. She trembles all over. She has trouble feeding herself. But she called me a real man. Not just a good man, like Charlie Brown, who's sad and sorry all the time, but a *real* man. This is the closest I've come to having my own side of the mountain.

"Will you run away with me?" I ask the granny.

"Let's get the hell out of here," she says, giggling and nibbling on her fries.

twenty-three

My mother and I shop at Sears for a new pair of jeans and sneakers for me. "As an early Christmas present," she says. There's a Korean adage that says if you buy shoes for someone as a gift, you're really telling him to run away. *Put these new shoes on and get lost.*

My mother gets enough kimchi orders that she doesn't have to sew sleeves or work on the weekends at Arirang Grocery anymore. Word got around about her kimchi, and people who don't even go to our church are ordering jars. Our home has gone from being a sewing factory to a kimchi factory.

While her kimchi business grows, my braiding business is steady but slow. I've managed to save forty-two dollars. I was thinking about giving it to my mother, but it doesn't look like she needs the money anymore.

My mother pays for my sneakers, then wanders over to the women's clothing department. I wander over to sporting goods. As I leave the aisle of fishing rods, I see the most amazing display. A family of mannequins is camping. The dad stands next to the tent, which is as big as a real house and is a color Crayola calls Shamrock. The boy stands near the fire, made out of jagged pieces of red cardboard. The girl stands with her mom, who's boiling water in a kettle that sits on a portable stove the size of a dictionary. The Styrofoam snow is pure and beautiful. The family is frozen in a moment of happiness.

I carefully walk over to the tent, push open the flap, and look inside. Four puffy sleeping bags are lined up on the floor. I step into the tent, zipper shut the door, and then, like Goldilocks, try out all the sleeping bags. The boy's green one is just right. I am cocooned. The air smells fresh, like brand-new shower curtains. The tent's ceiling glows green from the store's fluorescent lights and hypnotizes me: *You're getting sleepy. You're getting a tent. Your own home. Your hollow tree.*

"Assistance needed in shoes."

The voice, which sounds like the school secretary's, springs me out of the sleeping bag. I bolt out of the tent like I'm escaping a crime scene.

I hurry to the aisle of tents, which are boxed and shelved according to size. The smallest is a two-person tent called the Shelter 365. Lightweight but tough. No stakes needed. Erects quickly. Durable mesh window and door. Nylon wraparound floor to keep out moisture and bugs. Cost: $59.99.

I want the Shelter 365. I need the Shelter 365. Without it, there is no way to escape. I must run away. Dump before you get dumped. Leave before you get kicked out. It's inevitable. Deacon Koh is on his way in, and I'm on my way out. My mother doesn't need me anymore. And with the Shelter 365, I won't need her.

twenty-four

Mickey's bedroom is filled with trophies, ribbons, tiaras, and pictures of her wearing lots of makeup, fancy dresses, and Dolly Parton hairdos. When she was little, she competed in pageants. She really was Miss America.

"My daddy was all into it, and I'd do anything for my daddy 'cause he truly believed in his heart of hearts that I could be Miss America, so he started me real young, putting me in every pageant on Earth and hooting and hollering in the audience when I did my signature strut. Ma hated it, thought it was the biggest waste of money and time, and they fought about it like cats and dogs," she says, and stands up to look at herself in the mirror. "You know that girl Lenore?"

"No," I say.

"That girl lie to my face. She promise she do the talent show with me, then she say her mama won't let her roller-skate onstage 'cause it's too dangerous and she don't want her breaking any bones, so I tell her we could just dance instead without the skates, but she say she can't do the talent show period 'cause it's against her religion, then I see her singing with some other girls during recess. Religion, my butt cheeks. I know they getting ready for the talent show. I hate Lenore. I want to roller-skate over her throat. I heard that girl sing, and believe you me, that girl can't sing. Worst part is she think she sound good, and she sing real loud and with all this feeling that only make her face look constipated. If she don't get kicked out by them girls, she gonna get laughed at by the whole school and not in the good kind of way," Mickey says.

"Is it hard?" I ask, wondering if I might replace Lenore. I still have no act for the talent show, and there's a hundred bucks at stake, and I've seen Mickey skate. I figure she can dance in her skates, while I just stand onstage. It'd be the fastest and easiest fifty I've ever made.

"Is what hard?"

"You know, skating."

"At first it is, but then you practice, and you get the hang of it," she says. "Why? You want to learn to skate?"

"I don't know. I really suck at stuff like that," I say, shrugging and looking down at my feet in hopes of winning her encouragement.

"If you think you suck, then I guess you suck," she says.

"That's not exactly what I was getting at."

"I know what you were trying to get at, and I'm saying I refuse to have as my talent show partner somebody who thinks he sucks. I can teach the skating part, but I can't teach the attitude part. If you think you suck, I, the teacher, ain't got nothing to work with," she says, amazing me into silence.

Mickey's door opens, and a boy's face squeezes in the crack. A gray cat slithers in, meowing. It comes to me and rubs against my ankles, making eights between my legs. I feel nervous. I lean against the dresser just in case it knocks me down.

"What you want?" Mickey says.

"I wanna play," the boy says.

"Not now, Benny. Can't you see? I got a guest."

He sticks his tongue out at her.

"Keep that tongue out another nanosecond and I'm cutting it off," she says, and throws a pillow at him.

Her brother runs off, leaving the door wide open. Mickey shuts it. "I swear. A girl can't get no privacy round here. Ain't that right, Jill?" she says, petting the cat. She sits on the floor, and Jill steps into the diamond nest formed by Mickey's legs and settles in. She strokes its neck. The cat growls.

"You scared a cats?" she asks me.

"No," I say.

"Sit down. Pet her. Jill ain't going to bite. She loves this, but don't pet Kelly. He's the orange one. He's grumpy. He don't want to be touched. Daddy says he's mad at us for giving him a girl name. See? She don't bite," Mickey says.

"She's growling," I say, pulling my hand away.

"That's purring."

"Is she mad?"

"She's happy. Cats purr 'cause they're happy."

"Oh yeah, I knew that," I say, and return to petting the cat.

I actually don't know much about cats. I've never heard a cat purr before. I didn't even know cats made a sound other than the annoying meow, which reminds me of whining and squeaky doors. Purring is entirely different. The sound doesn't seem to come out of her mouth. It comes from some deep place inside and vibrates all over. It's steady and even, as long as I keep up with the petting. I don't want to take my hand away because I don't want the purring to end.

"Wanna see a trick?" Mickey asks, and picks up the cat. She wears Jill around her neck the way athletes wear towels around their necks. The cat's legs hang down on either side.

"Cool," I say.

"Wanna try?" she asks, pulling the cat carefully off. Before I can answer no, she drapes the cat around my neck, resting her on my shoulders. Her weight and warmth feel good. The fur brushes against my cheeks and ears. No wonder some women are crazy about fur coats. I sink into the comfort and turn my head from side to side, feeling the fur on my face.

"You wanna ask me something," she says.

"Ask you what?"

"Beating around the bush don't suit you. Ask already."

"Ask what?"

"I gotta be the one to spell out the desires of your heart? Can't you ask for yourself?"

"Ask what?"

"Repeat after me. Mickey. Say my name. Say 'Mickey.'"

"Mickey," I say.

"Will you," she says.

"Will you," I repeat.

"Marry me," she says, and laughs out loud. Still chuckling, she says, "No. No, I'm just kidding. You should've seen the look on your face. No, but this time it's serious. For real. Repeat after me. Will you . . ."

"Will you," I say.

"Show me," she says.

"Show me."

"How to roller-skate good like you do so I can be your partner in the talent show and we can kick some Lenore butt and win this thing?" she says.

"Okay. Yeah. That," I say.

"Under one condition. As long as you recognize that I am the true star in this partnership and that you are the one riding my coattails," she says, fists on her hips.

"And we split the prize money fifty-fifty?"

"Fifty-fifty. I don't care about the money. I just want the glory of winning. I am so sick and tired of them making fun of me. They got no idea what I have inside. No idea. For once I want them to see me do something I'm good at and sit there admiring me and wishing to be like me, even for a split second. Is that so much to ask for? Well, you in or not?" she demands, her voice about to crack.

"I'm in," I say, and put out my hand, sweating under the weight and warmth of the cat draped around my neck.

"Put it here, partner? Oh my Lordy, you are the corniest. You wanna spit in our hands to seal the deal like they do in the movies?" Mickey says, shaking my hand. Her hand feels damp.

"But I don't have skates, and I don't know how to skate," I say.

"You could use my old pair," she says, and hurries out of the room, leaving me on her bedroom floor yoked by the cat. I feel hot. I feel chills. How do I get this cat off me? I lower my head to the floor, hoping she'll step off and move along, but she stays put. Mickey returns with a pair of black roller skates. I feel strangely disappointed they aren't red, white, and blue like hers.

"Try them on," she says as she lifts the cat off me.

"They're too small."

"Your feet ain't as big as you think. Now put them on," she says, and pulls my sneakers off. I curl my toes so she can't push my foot into the skate.

"I'll show you," she says, tickling my foot.

"Stop!" I say, suppressing a giggle. My toes relax, and she pushes my foot into the skate. It fits.

"Let me make it clear to you that I have never skated in my life."

"That's fine. You'll get it. It's so easy-peasy," she says, tightly lacing up the skate.

"I don't know about this."

Mickey double-knots the laces and says, "If you get any doubts about yourself, just think about the money. Keep your eye on the money. I know about you, Ok. I know how much you love money. Just think about all you can do with all that cash."

Winning the talent show would get me the Shelter 365 with change to spare. I could stop braiding.

"Stand up," Mickey says. I stand. She presses her thumb on the toes of the skates the way my mother does when checking the fit of my shoes. The skates feel good and snug on my feet. For once in my life, I feel tall.

twenty-five

My mother practices her signature on a napkin at Burger King with Deacon Koh's gold pen. He sits across from us at a booth, shuffling through sheets of paper in a folder labeled HOME BENEFICIAL LIFE INSURANCE COMPANY.

My mother nods as he explains death benefit, cash value, interest rates, future insurability, premium cost, and beneficiary.

As my mother signs the papers without reading them, the deacon smiles, leans in to her, and says, "Praise the Lord. Think about the peace of mind this brings. You don't have to worry about the future anymore. Who's hungry?" he asks, rubbing his hands together.

I don't answer. My mother elbows me. I reluctantly play along by raising my hand and saying, "Me."

"No problemo. Ok looks like he wants a Whopper with onion rings," the deacon says.

"Oh boy, how did you know?" I say in monotone.

"I know these things. I, too, was once a growing young man with a big appetite," he says, and goes to order our food.

"Be nice," my mother whispers.

"Ŏmma, you didn't even read those papers. You don't even know what you signed," I whisper.

"I don't need to. He explained everything to me," she says.

"But what if he's lying?" I ask.

"The deacon doesn't lie. He cares about us," she says.

"No, he doesn't," I say.

"I trust him," she says.

"I don't," I say.

My mother is quiet. Her lips tighten. She shoves the papers at me and says, "Then here! Read them yourself! You think I'm so dumb I'll sign our lives over to just anyone? I don't understand you sometimes. The deacon has been so helpful. He's been nothing but kind and generous to you, and you with your 'okay, okay, okay' and rolling eyes is so disrespectful. What's wrong with you?" she demands, her volume rising.

"Nothing," I say.

"Give me a real answer," she says.

"He tries too hard," I say.

"Of course he's trying hard. He wants you to like him. What's wrong with that?" she says, her teeth clenched.

"I don't like it," I say.

"Then would you rather he not take you out with us and feed you? Would you rather we have you wait in the car while we eat? Would you rather we ignore you and treat you like you're nothing but a big bother and nuisance and burden?" she says.

Deacon Koh brings a tray of food and drinks with a big smile and says, "So, what's this I hear about you not knowing how to swim, Ok? That's an important life skill. I can teach you. No problemo. I have a membership at the YMCA. I'm going to take you with me and teach you how to swim. No drowning accidents allowed on my watch, no, indeed."

I try hard to hold back tears. To keep from crying, I bite into the Whopper, chew, and swallow to clear the lump in my throat. My legs shake under the table. My mother and the deacon sit face-to-face, unwrapping their sandwiches. They pour their two orders of onion rings onto the tray into one pile so they can share. How cute. They're a pair. They're a couple. To keep from throwing up, I stuff my mouth with onion rings. I gulp down my Coke, trying to douse the burn inside. It's not heartburn. It's a mad ache in my chest. I can't breathe. I think I'm choking. I clear my throat. I cough. I can't stop coughing.

"Go. Excuse yourself," my mother says.

As I keep coughing, I get up and walk out of Burger King. I stand in the parking lot coughing like a smoker, which keeps me from crying and feeling hurt. I find my father's car and sit on the hood, which still feels warm from the heat of the engine. I press my knuckles into the metal, promising myself to get the hell out of here.

twenty-six

Mickey comes up with the idea of practicing at the empty pool. We climb the fence with skates in backpacks. I get over easily. Mickey has a harder time, but she does it, and we run down the steps into the concrete box until we come to the deeper end. Eleven feet deep. We stand there among the fallen sticks and leaves and look up at the sky, its clouds as pretty as the ones in once-upon-a-time-happily-ever-after storybooks.

The pool has a large, open space. A smooth surface. Four walls to keep me from colliding with cars and dying and rolling down to hell. And most importantly, no one to see us.

"Hurry, get on the skates," she whispers loudly, taking her shoes off and emptying her backpack.

Mickey looks nervous. As she laces her skates, her hands tremble from the cold, the excitement, the fear. If we get caught, we could end up in jail for trespassing, but I'm not scared. Sure, my heart beats faster than usual and my hands get clammy, but I feel alert and alive and ready. Go ahead. Call me names. Spit in my face. Trip me. Laugh. Leave me out. Leave me behind. I'm fine. I'm fighting back. When you least expect it, I'm going to get you. I'm going to win.

Mickey skates in circles like she knows what she's doing, her hair teased into a mess. She controls and directs the spinning wheels. She looks composed, balanced, and confident, like she dances to a secret song playing in her head. She's good, really good. Whatever jitters Mickey had coming down here, she skates them away. She does a fancy turn, stops right in front of me, and says, "Stop staring, Goo-Goo Eyes. Skate. Show me what you got."

"I don't have anything. Like I told you, I stink at this," I say.

It takes a great deal of effort, strength, and concentration on my part to keep from falling. I consider standing without collapsing a personal accomplishment. Please do not ask me to move.

"You gotta move," she says.

"Why?"

"'Cause you're gonna look stupid, and you're gonna make me look stupid, and we ain't winning with us looking stupid," she says, and takes my hand.

"Wait. Wait," I say, pulling my hand away. "I have

an idea. What if we make me like a robot or a scarecrow or a statue or even a rock? I'll just stand still in a rock costume, and you could do your skating-dancing thing around me, and let's say you're skating-dancing around the rock and doing all your moves because you want the rock to turn into a prince, yeah, but it doesn't really work out and the whole thing ends up very sad in the end because you give up and stop skating and just die next to the rock because you're so tired because you skated yourself to death and that's when the rock takes off his costume and it turns out that the rock transforms into a prince but it's too late, since you died, and the prince sees that you died so he just turns back into a rock," I say.

"What the heckers? We ain't doing some Romeo-Juliet nonsense. Oh my Lordy, that is so depressing. You wanna get booed off the stage?" she says, and takes my hand again.

Mickey pulls me. I roll, my free arm stretched out for balance. Help. I'm petrified. My body is bent over and locked at a 135-degree angle. My butt sticks out as if searching for a toilet. I am forever frozen in the about-to-vomit-about-to-potty position.

Just as I'm getting the hang of being rolled along, Mickey releases me across the pool. I skate. Actually, I roll. Right into a wall. I ricochet off the white wall of death, my arms forming big and useless circles to defy gravity. My feet don't help. I back-shuffle for as long as I can. Then I fall.

As Mickey skates over to me, she says, "The most important thing is to overcome your fear of falling, because that fear is going to keep you from skating or trying anything else in life. But as long as you can face that fear and let yourself fall, and fall properly, 'cause there's a right way to fall and a wrong way to fall, then you are bound to win. Ok, you good at falling. You did it right. You landed on your butt. You got nothing to be afraid of. You're a natural. As long as you fall on your butt, knees, hands, anywhere but your head, then you doing it right."

I get up, steady myself, brush off the leaves, and say, "I'm okay."

"It's just like walking. One foot in front of the other," she says.

I straighten my back. I take small steps, one foot in front of the other. I don't try to roll. I don't try to go fast. It takes a while, but I make it to the other side of the pool. Mickey holds out her palm for a five. As I smack her a five, I fall again. But I get up and take my steps.

"You got that part down. Now give your steps a little push," she says.

I do. I give my steps a little push, and I'm slowly

skating from wall to wall. I fall a few more times, but I get up and keep going. Before I know it, I'm skating back and forth without falling as much.

"Keep at it! You doing it," she says, and skates uphill toward the shallow end of the pool. When she gets to the top, she squats down and pushes off with her hands. She rolls slowly at first. Then she picks up speed, gliding down the slope toward the deep end. Her hair blows away from her face. Her cheeks are splotched red. Her eyes are wide open with surprise.

"I'm going again," she says, and heads back to the top.

I can't skate up the incline, so I crawl my way to the shallow end. It's a long way down. What if I crash into the wall, breaking all my bones and splattering blood all over? I squat and push off. As the wheels spin and I pick up speed, my stomach gets that nervous sinking feeling of butterflies fluttering. I can't breathe. The wind blows. The white wall emerges out of the ground. Mickey waves from the bottom. Is she going to catch me?

"Fall! Fall!" she yells.

I wrap my arms around my head and let myself fall, tumbling the rest of the way down and landing at the skates of a cheering Mickey.

On my back, I look up. The clouds move in the gray December sky. Six more days until Christmas. The air is cold and fresh. My throat feels dry. My heart beats fast.

Mickey's head pops into view and hovers over me, blocking the sky. She says, "You all right?"

"Yeah," I say, and sit up.

"That was wild," she says.

"Yeah," I say, and unlace the skates.

"I ain't got no doubt in my mind and in my heart of hearts that you will be ready for the talent show, and we are going to win that thing," she says, taking off her skates.

"Whatever you say."

"My daddy's going to be there, hooting and hollering and whistling at us. He can blow the best whistles. They're the loudest I ever heard. It's the kind where you stick your fingers in your mouth and blow. He tried to teach me once, but I can't do it. Is your mama and daddy coming?" she says.

"They wouldn't miss it for the world," I say, feeling a sudden pang inside, like hunger that hurts. I wish my father had had lessons in falling.

We throw the backpacks over the fence, and they land on the grass. We climb over and head home.

"Where you come from again?" Mickey asks.

"Korea," I say.

"That's far away, ain't it?"

"I guess."

"You got any brothers and sisters?"

"No."

"Lucky duck. Wish I was an only child."

"I don't know. It's kind of boring."

"I guess so," she says, and walks toward her apartment.

"Bye. Thanks for not laughing at me," I say.

"We still got a lot of work to do. Tomorrow is another day," she calls out, and disappears into her building.

After I pass her apartment, I take off my shoes and put on Mickey's old skates again and practice by skating home. One foot in front of the other. Give each step a little push. Stand tall and straight. No fear of falling. I keep thinking about my father falling. Was he afraid? Did he know there was a right way and a wrong way to fall? What if he'd tucked himself into a ball? What if he'd rolled as he landed? What if?

Then I wouldn't be here skating toward the Shelter 365 with plans of running away.

twenty-seven

Deacon Koh wears an orange Speedo that's so tight I can't stop thinking about clementines and wishing Mickey came along so we could make fun of him. He also wears a matching orange swim cap with the black stripes of a tiger. I try not to stand near him. My trunks aren't real swimming trunks. They're a pair of old shorts that balloon as I climb down the ladder into the water. I flatten them out, and they hang heavy on my waist. Deacon Koh puts on his goggles and swims to the other end, showing off his stuff and leaving me at the wall. With me on my tiptoes, the water comes to my chin. I make my way toward the shallow end, where mothers wear their children on their backs, hips, and shoulders. The water is surprisingly warm. Koh swims toward me. Staying afloat, he asks, "Are you ready for your first lesson?"

I shake my head no.

"Don't be scared. This is very easy. This is very

natural. When we're relaxed and calm and trusting in God, our bodies naturally float. But when we are full of fear and doubt and anxiety, our bodies tighten up, and we sink and drown. The first rule in swimming is to relax and trust in God. Then the second rule is to get your head wet. You have to get used to getting your face wet. Put your head in the water."

"No thanks," I say.

"It's so easy. You can do it," he says.

"No," I say.

"It's like taking a bath. Hold your breath and go under. Try it," he says, taking a breath and dunking his head under. He swims closer to me and looks like he's about to grab my ankle and pull me under, so I kick and step away. He emerges from the water dripping wet like a tiger fish.

"Being comfortable putting your face in the water is the first step, the foundation to learning how to swim. You have to build a strong foundation. The Bible says that if you build a house on sand, that house will collapse, so you must build your house on stone, so it can withstand wind and storms," he says.

"Okay," I say, wondering what the Bible has to do with swimming. If anything, more people in the Bible drown than swim.

He slaps the water, splashing me, laughing.

I say, "Stop." I turn around, covering my face. He continues to splash my back, and I get annoyed. I turn around and splash him back.

"Oh yeah? Show what you got," he says in English, and splashes me back.

We splash each other. Koh's laughter echoes throughout the indoor pool. The lifeguard blows his whistle and says, "No splashing."

"No problemo," he says to the lifeguard, and I want to disappear in the water.

"Your face is all wet. Put your head under. Is no difference," he says.

"No," I say.

"Are you like a chicken?" he says.

"Are you serious?" I say.

"Oh, berry, berry serious," he says, grabs my head, dunks me under, and holds me there. I can't breathe. I flail in the water. I open my eyes. I reach for Koh's glow-underwater Speedo, but my arms move in slow motion.

He lets go. I stand. I breathe. With water up my nose and in my ears and eyes, I cough. I taste chlorine. My entire head stings, and I want to punch Koh so hard that his rubber head explodes like an overinflated balloon, but instead I whine, "Why'd you do that?"

"Do you know how I learned to swim? I was five years old, and my father took me to a lake and threw me in. I figured it out all by myself. Swimming is very natural. Your body knows how to do it already. You have to give it the chance. You have to overcome your fears. Ok, you have so many fears. I can tell. But you have to face and overcome them or you will remain a chicken. A chicken is a terrible bird. It can't even fly. It's only good for eating. You can't be a chicken anymore. Don't you want to be a tiger? Proud, powerful, and courageous. Now put your mouth and nose in like this and blow bubbles," he says.

I do what he says and blow bubbles.

"Every time your head goes in the water, you have to breathe out hard so the water doesn't come inside your face. Breathe out hard like you're blowing your nose. Later, when I teach you how to swim freestyle, I'll show you the breathing rhythm, but for now you need to practice blowing bubbles when your head goes under," he says.

"Fine," I say.

"Now I will teach you how to float. Floating is the easiest and the hardest part about swimming. Do you remember how I said having a strong foundation is so very important? Floating is the foundation to swimming. This is the part where you must trust in God.

Trust that you will be carried. You must be relaxed. If you're tense and scared, your muscles will get tight and heavy and you will drown," he says, and supports me with one hand while tipping me back with the other, as if lowering me into a coffin.

I can't stand looking up at him. Deacon Koh looks like a monster. I close my eyes, spread out my arms and legs, listen to the echo of voices and splashes coming from where the mothers and children play. I give up. I relax. I float. I move along the water until my head bumps against a rope. I open my eyes. The deacon is nowhere near me. Trying to stay relaxed, I stare up at the ceiling, where steel beams crisscross into a tangle of webs, and wonder what the next rule of swimming might be, wonder if the deacon has left me to float away so he can have my mother to himself. I float and move my arms slowly, steering myself toward the ladder. I climb out, my wet shorts heavy around my waist. I hold them up as I hobble to my towel.

Wrapped in a towel and shivering, I sit and look for the deacon. His orange-and-black tiger head glides across the surface of the water, angling every four strokes for air. As I watch him swim laps, I feel doomed. The more I think about it, the more it makes sense. He has a motive. There's mounting evidence, however circumstantial. Whenever I ride in the car with him, he never tells me to put on my seat belt like he does with my mother, and when he gives me water to drink, I swear I smell Clorox, and when he gives me food to eat, I smell gasoline. On top of that, he made me go on a walk with him in the woods, just the two of us, and picked a mushroom from the ground, lecturing me on the fungus's nutritional benefits and how to identify poisonous ones. He assured me the one in his hand was not poisonous, perfectly safe to eat.

"Try it. You'll grow tall and strong."

"No thanks. I'm not hungry."

"No problemo."

Like one mushroom would transform me into an NBA player. And he keeps promising to take me to Ocean City once the weather warms up. Why take a nonswimmer to the ocean, where there are sharks and where the depth of the water shifts with each oncoming wave, sucking you into the mouth of the sea, farther and farther away from the shore? Is Deacon Koh attempting to murder me?

I throw the towel over my head and rub my hair dry, telling myself to stop jumping to conclusions. I'm thinking crazy. Why do I dislike him so much? He tries too hard, and trying too hard shows desperation. He's hiding something. I don't trust him. He's messing with my mother. She used to like me. She used to be nice to me. We were doing just fine before he came along with his self-righteous sermons, life insurance policies, and no-problemo fast food. Who does he think he is? My father?

twenty-eight

My hands are freezing. To warm them up, I tuck my fingers into Danielle's curly hair. Her head feels warm. Our class is outside for recess, and unless you're playing basketball, chasing squirrels, or doing jumping jacks, it's impossible to warm up. We hide behind a shrub, Danielle squatting in front of me. My hands reluctantly pull away from her warm head, divide a portion of her hair into three, and start to braid. I'm halfway done when my nose starts to run. Snot drips. I sniffle, but the snot's too much and too far gone. As the goo slides to my mouth, I press my lips tightly together. I'm not about to eat my boogers. The snot drips down my chin and onto Danielle's hair. I'm sorry, but I keep braiding. Maybe this'll be my best braid yet. Maybe this'll be my secret braiding ingredient.

After I tie the end of the braid, I quickly wipe my face on the cuff of my jacket. As Danielle pays me with four quarters and takes off, a basketball rolls toward me. I stop it with my foot and pick it up. Asa shows up, looking for the ball. He sniffles. His nose drips like mine. He wipes it with the cuff of his jacket. With all my force and accuracy, I throw the ball at him. He catches it. He dribbles it, eyeing me between bounces, making sure I'm watching him show off. I sniffle, wipe my nose, and start to walk away, when Asa snaps the ball back to me with such precision that it magically appears between my hands. He tilts his head, pointing it to the court, and says, "We short, man. You in?"

"Me?"

"Yeah, you."

"Me?"

"Get over here 'fore I rewind," he says.

I play basketball with Asa and his friends, and it's not a humiliating disaster. I guess I'm running and dribbling and passing the ball. I must be. It's a blurry fantasy. I'm sweaty and out of breath. I'm not making any baskets, but when I get the ball (it's more like when the ball gets to me), I do exactly what my father said and pass it to the one who can make baskets, Asa. He scores, high-fives me, and I wonder, Wait. Is this really happening?

The bell rings.

As the rest of the class runs inside, Asa tugs the

back of my collar. He motions with the tilt of his head to follow him to the end of the line. When we get there, he puts his arm around me like I belong to him. He smells like dirty laundry. His breath streams out of his mouth into the cold air like smoke from a dragon. I wriggle out of his hold and say, "What do you want?"

The rejection takes him by surprise. His feelings are hurt. He struggles to talk. His frustration returns him to his normal self. He nudges me the way a piñata gets handled before the beating. The rest of the class is in the building, and I don't want trouble from Asa or the teacher, so before he calls me Chingy-Chongy or burps in my face, I hurry to the doors and call out, "I got it. I'll keep quiet."

He catches up and says, "'Bout what?"

"I don't know what you're talking about," I say.

"You the man," he says, and pats my head.

As we walk through the hall to the classroom, Asa gives me the silent *You're so stupid* laugh and covers his mouth with one hand and points a finger at me with the other. I sniffle and wipe my face. He sniffles and wipes his face, mocking me as usual, but this time he seems almost sorry and embarrassed about it. As we near the classroom, Asa limp-struts close by and hovers over me like a clinging shadow. He acts like his time is running out. He hunches down as if to confess, and with the unmoving lips of a ventriloquist, he whispers, "You smart, ain't you?"

"I guess," I say, shrugging.

"You good at reading," he says.

"I guess," I say.

"You good enough to teach?" he asks.

"I guess," I say.

"'Cause I got this friend . . . ," he says, limp-strutting into the classroom. He looks at me over his shoulder and smiles slyly.

twenty-nine

I agree to tutor Asa in reading and writing, and I draw up a contract, just to be safe.

Price: twenty dollars (50 percent down payment at the first lesson and the remaining balance to be collected at the final lesson, when literacy is achieved). Money-back guarantee.

Number of lessons: five (more or less, depending on the client's commitment, discipline, and work ethic).

Location: Public library is ideal, but the client expresses concerns. He fears risk of exposure, so we agree to meet in the woods behind my father's dream house. (The Shelter 365 would come in handy.) If weather conditions do not permit, the lesson will be held in the client's home.

Materials: Client will provide all notebooks, paper, and pencils. Instructor will provide all learning materials in the form of flash cards, books, and work sheets.

We sign the contract on the dotted lines. Asa prints

his name, the *s* shaped into a lightning bolt separating the two *a*'s. As soon as I put down my well-practiced John Hancock with the roller-coastered, loop-the-looped "Lee," I recognize my father's signature, which used to authorize and bear witness to all my excellent report cards. I used to practice his signature, tracing his lines and memorizing his curves, just in case I got a bad grade or he wasn't around. I fold up the contract and put out my hand. Asa shakes it. A real business deal. Man-to-man.

thirty

I wait for Mickey on her couch. I need to learn the dance moves.

The dog, Charlie, sits at my feet and looks at me, sniffing the air between us. We get into a staring contest. Just as I'm about to blink, Charlie looks away. As I privately celebrate my victory, the dog jumps onto the couch and sniffs my ear. I freeze, hoping my imitation of a statue bores him enough to give up and go away. He sniffs more aggressively, as if my stillness is a challenge to smell me back into motion. I get scared. Knowing dogs get excited when they detect fear, I get even more scared. I stop breathing, just in case the dog smells fear on my breath. Please don't lick me. Charlie licks me. His tongue, wet and warm, rubs across my face like a slow-motion slap of affection. I stand up, wiping my cheeks. He looks at me, wagging his tail, tilting his head, and panting. *What's the matter? We were having so much fun.* I point at him with a trembling, unconvincing finger and feebly tell him to stop.

Charlie jumps off the couch, stands on his hind legs, and pushes me down. I fall in submission, roly-poly into a ball, and let the dog have his way with me.

"Let's get down. It's boogie time," Mickey announces.

"Help," I say.

"Dumb dog, get! Get off him," she says.

Mickey grabs Charlie by the collar, drags him into a room, shuts the door, and shouts, "Benny, you best not be disturbing us while we rehearsing. I swear, you do and your face is getting rubbed in that litter box, and it ain't been cleaned out in forever."

Mickey sashays into the living room and twirls, exposing her underwear, except I think she's wearing a one-piece bathing suit underneath her skirt, like the leotards dancers wear, which makes seeing it okay, I guess, because it isn't really underwear. She stops in front of the Christmas tree, places her hands on her waist, swings her hips back and forth, and demands, "Bow down before my badness. How do I look?"

Her faded pink bathing suit is too tight. Her gauzy pink skirt looks like it's made from an old lady's night-gown. Her hair is huge, teased up even more than usual. Her eyes are shaded blizzard blue. Her cheeks are blushed in streaks of sunset orange. Her lips are smeared in scarlet red. Halloween comes to mind, but I say, "Fine."

She twirls to the CD player and turns on "Stayin' Alive" by the Bee Gees. The music turns Mickey into a puppet, the song's beat pulling and tugging at her. She knows how to dance. While she's stayin' alive, I'm stayin' dead still. I don't dance. I don't know how. I sit down on the couch and say, "This isn't going to work. We're not going to win. This song's too old. No one's going to recognize it."

"No one but all the teachers! And guess who is judging? Thanks to us, they going to have themselves a blast from the past. Now get up," Mickey says, grabs me, and stands me up in front of her. She holds my limp hands and swings my arms, telling me to copy her feet. Step left. Bring feet together. Step right. Bring feet together. Left. Together. Right. Together.

"Keep going. That's good. You're gettin' it. Move to the beat. Not like that! You're way too stiff. Pretend you're like liquid, all loose and relaxed. Come on, Ok. You gotta loosen up. Close your eyes. Listen to the music," she says, sounding frustrated.

I close my eyes and step left-together-right-together, listening for the beat, pretending to be liquid, and trying to loosen up to the Bee Gees whining about life going nowhere.

I think I'm getting the hang of it, but Mickey says, "I don't know. Something's not right. This ain't going to work." She steps away from me like my lack of rhythm is a contagious disease, and stops the CD.

"What's wrong with you? Are you deaf or something?" she asks, planting a fist on her hip. The red lipstick looks like blood. "This is serious, Ok. We ain't got much time."

"I told you. I can't dance," I say.

"Baloney. Everyone can dance. It's natural. It's like breathing. All of nature dances. You ever see birds flying or fish swimming or leaves blowing in the wind? That's all dancing. You just gotta move and flow and let it happen to you," she says, moving her arms like she's conducting an orchestra.

"Actually, deaf people can dance. They may not hear the music, but they feel vibrations," I say.

"Well, Bingo was his name-o. There you go. Feel the vibrations in the air," she says, and looks into my eyes, threatening me with cat-litter facials.

Once upon a time, I saw my mother and father dancing in the living room. They danced the way old people dance, arms holding each other, cheek to cheek, swaying together, slowly spinning in circles, lost in the motion and the music. I think Elvis was crooning. I watched them for a minute, but soon my hands and feet got sweaty like I was about to get in trouble, so I left because I didn't belong there, there was no room for me, that was private and none of my business. I wonder if my mother dances with the deacon.

There is money to be won. There is a tent to be bought. There is an escape to be made. I must dance.

Mickey plays the song again and tells me to copy her. Follow the groove. Feel the vibrations. The room vibrates. The tree lights blink out of beat with the lighted wings of the angel on top. A cat jumps on the couch, sits on the middle cushion, and watches me point to the ceiling-floor-ceiling-floor, my arm swinging diagonally across my chest. The belt of a safety patrol uniform comes to mind. Just as I think I'm getting the hang of it, I see Mickey, lost in her enjoyment, and realize I'm far from dancing; I'm directing traffic.

Half of Benny's face pops out from behind the kitchen wall. He watches my moves and cries out, "He's a robot. He's a robot."

Mickey stops dancing and looks at Benny. She looks at me. She looks at Benny again. I want to tell him to run because she's going to suffocate him in the litter box. She lunges toward him, squeezes his face, kisses him on the forehead, and says, "You, Benny-Boy, are my little genius." She turns to me and proclaims, "Ok, you are going to dance the robot. You look like one. You probably smell like one. And no doubt about it, you dance like one." She congratulates herself by popping her head like a robot and asks, "Think you can do it?"

Am I not the genius who first suggested I play a tree, statue, rock, or robot? Wasn't she the one who rejected the idea? I let her take the credit and bask in the glory of her brilliance. What do I care? I'm relieved I don't have to move like liquid. I hold my arms at ninety-degree angles, bow stiffly, pop my head up, and answer, "Affirmative."

thirty-one

Thanks to the all-you-can-drink Cokes at Alario's Pizzeria, I have to pee like crazy in the middle of the Christmas Eve service when Pastor Chung preaches about being thirsty for righteousness and seeking spiritual water found only in Jesus. I dash out of the sanctuary and head for the men's room.

Passing an office with its door slightly ajar, I catch sight of the back of a familiar burgundy tweed sport jacket. I know that jacket because during dinner I noted how stupid it looks over the green shirt and red tie, Deacon Koh's festive holiday attire. Full bladdered, I pause at the office door that should be shut and locked. I peek in because Deacon Koh stands with his back to the door and can't see me seeing him.

He stands before a table covered with silver offering plates that overflow with envelopes, checks, and cash. The spoils of Christmas Eve. It's the deacon's job to count the offering money, but he's alone tonight. No one counts the offering alone. It's against church rules. I have to go before I wet my pants, but I see what I see: Deacon Koh slips bills into the left pocket of his burgundy tweed sport jacket. As if I'm the thief, I make a run for it.

thirty-two

With no faith in Santa and the promise of going to the d-CON's house, I want to sleep through Christmas morning. Yes, d-CON, as in the mousetrap that kills the helpless, the unwanted.

When my mother tells me to wake up because he's going to be here any minute to pick us up, I fake-cough, shiver, and say my stomach hurts. To check my temperature, she puts a hand on my cheek and presses her right eye on my forehead, a gesture that always makes me feel better even if I'm burning up with a fever. She holds her eye there, searching for heat, searching for the truth. "You're not sick," she says, and pulls the blanket off me.

"My stomach hurts," I say.

"Santa brought you a present," she says, pulling my arm.

My parents were never good at playing Santa. They wrapped my presents in Korean newspaper. They signed the cards in Korean. Santa was from the North Pole; he was not Korean. My father explained that Santa was of all races and knew all languages. I never bought it.

My mother drags me out of bed and to the living room, where there's a box covered in laughing pink Santa faces. If I were giving a gift, I would never use wrapping paper that has my laughing face plastered all over it. I tear the paper off and open the box. Nestled in tissue paper are a pair of shiny brown shoes, the kind you wear to church and funerals. Under the shoes are a shirt, a tie, and a three-piece suit the same shade of burgundy as the d-CON's jacket from last night.

"Oh! Look what Santa brought you! Look at those shoes! So shiny. Is that real leather? Look at that suit! How handsome! Grandfather Santa Claus was thinking about you this year. Hurry, go put them on," she says.

"Now?"

"Now," she says.

"Shouldn't I save these for a special occasion?"

"Today is special! Hurry. Put your new clothes on. The deacon's going to be here any minute," she says, and pushes the gifts at me.

I get dressed. Everything is too big. Everything feels heavy and itchy. The clip-on tie keeps falling off the loose collar of the baggy shirt. The shoes are big too. I drag myself out to show my mother how foolish I look, but she hugs me, bursts out, "You look so handsome! You're such a good son!" and cries.

"Ŏmma, don't cry," I say.

"Ok-ah, we suffered so much this year, but things are going to be better. I promise. You look so handsome. You're all grown up. From now on everything's going to be all right. I wish your father could've seen you like this," she says.

Appa would've laughed at me in this suit. He never liked getting dressed up. As soon as church was done and we were walking out of the building, he'd be pulling off his tie, undoing his shirt buttons, and lighting a cigarette.

"God has been very good to us, Ok. So many people have been very good to us, especially the deacon. I hope you're grateful. He cares about us. He takes you out to eat. He shows you how to be more spiritual. He teaches you how to swim. He really cares about you. I want you to think about him as more than a deacon from our church," she says.

"But, Ŏmma," I say.

"Think of him like he's part of our family, Ok," she says. "Like a father."

"Ŏmma, my stomach hurts."

"You're fine. It's all in your head," she says, straightening my tie. "You'll feel better. Let's have the best Christmas ever."

The best Christmas ever? Didn't we already have our best Christmas ever when Appa was alive? "Okay," I say, although this is not okay. I feel like throwing up.

"That's my good son," she says, patting my head. "You can meet the deacon's dog. He's a good dog. You'll like him. He'll follow you around everywhere."

"Do we have to go? Can't you just tell him we're busy today? I have a present for you," I say.

"You do?"

I go to my bed, reach underneath for the brown paper bag, bring it to her, and say, "Here. Merry Christmas."

She looks inside, smiles, and pulls out the new bottle of Jergens lotion I bought her. This one is legal. I purchased it with my own money. My mother looks in the bag again, sees what's at the bottom, looks up at me, and says, "Where did you get all this money?"

"I earned it doing some jobs at school. It should be more than enough to pay some of our bills," I say.

Her mouth is smiling, but her eyes look sad, like they're about to tear up. I want to tell her there's more where that came from, and see, we don't need the d-CON because I'm perfectly capable of taking care of us. I want her to say something that changes my mind about buying the Shelter 365 and running away. But she looks at me with pity and says, "The deacon will be here any minute."

There's a knock on the door.

thirty-three

assie is nothing like Mickey's dog, Charlie, who knocks me down and licks me at every chance and paces on the couch from arm to arm before spreading himself across the cushions. The d-CON's dog must've graduated at the top of his obedience class, because he obeys. When the d-CON commands him to sit, he sits. Stay. Roll. Turn in circles. Here. There. And all the commands are in Korean. I bet if the d-CON commanded him to attack me, he would.

While he and my mother are in the kitchen, I stand in front of the extra-large plastic Christmas tree, which is shrouded in gold tinsel and blinking with red lights. Because the ceiling is too low for the oversize tree, the angel on top is bent over like a hunchback and looming above me. In a silver ornament ball the size of a grapefruit I see Lassie's reflection. He stands at the doorway like a security guard, making sure I'm not touching or pocketing any of his master's treasures.

They turn down the volume of their laughter as they walk into the living room from the kitchen. My mother holds a tray of fruits, a cake, three cups, and a pitcher of red punch. The d-CON walks next to her, one hand holding a coffee mug and the other on my mother's back.

He tells me to take a sit, make myself a home. I hate it when he speaks English to me. I sit down on a chair next to the window and notice a dead fly on the sill. I look out. A squirrel scurries down a tree. It's in a panic, looking for the nuts it hid in the fall. I start to sweat underneath my new shirt, jacket, and tie, trying to figure out how I might go about making myself a home, my very own home.

They sit on the couch together. Lassie sits at the d-CON's feet. It's me on this side against them on that side. My mother takes a knife and taps an apple with its blade, making the first incision. As she peels the fruit, its red skin spirals off like a spool of ribbon. When I was younger, my mother peeling apples amazed me. She could pare them without breaking the long ribbon of skin. When she was done, I'd feel so proud of her and want to applaud and tell everyone, "Look what my mother can do." I can't seem to find that same pride right now.

The d-CON pours punch into a cup and sets it on

the corner of the table, expecting me to come and fetch it like a good little dog. I stay put. My mother plates slices of apples and a piece of pound cake and sets it next to the glass of punch.

"Ok-ah, here. Have some. Take your food," she says.

I don't move.

"I know he's hungry. He's always hungry. Isn't he being funny," she says, and bites into an apple slice.

I'm always hungry? What's that supposed to mean? And why is she talking about me like I'm not in the room? Am I shrinking? Am I disappearing? Is this monstrous three-piece suit swallowing me whole?

The d-CON stands up, goes to his fancy stereo, and plays a CD. It's Handel's *Messiah*.

My mother stands, picks up my plate of food, puts it on my lap, and places her hand on my forehead. Her hand feels warm and damp with apple juice. "He doesn't have a fever," she says, and walks away. I want to shrink down to the size of a safety pin, lie down on the slice of yellow pound cake, and sleep. Keeping the plate balanced on my knees, I watch the edges of the apple slices begin to brown.

The d-CON replaces my plate of food with a present, which is wrapped in the same laughing Santa paper the clothes and shoes came in. I slowly tear the paper. It's the Holy Bible bound in black leather, its onion-thin pages edged in gold. There are two ribbon bookmarkers attached on top, one for each testament, new and old.

The choir is singing, "For unto us a child is born, unto us a son is given . . ."

"That's too much. It looks so expensive. He loves books. Is that real gold? What do you say, Ok?" my mother says.

"Thank you," I manage, hoping he won't say "No problemo," because if he does, I'm going to throw the Bible at him.

"No problemo," he says.

The choir sings, the different parts echoing one another about the birth of a child.

"Oh no, I don't think he prepared a gift for you," my mother says.

"No problemo. I have everything I want right here. Children aren't supposed to give presents to their parents. Besides, it's far better to give than to receive. I'm not done yet. I have more to give. I have a very big and important gift to give this wonderful Christmas morning. I am giving you and your mother the gift of family. We will be a family. I've already asked your mother to marry me, and she happily agreed," he says.

With the choir singing about the government being upon his shoulder, my mother takes out a ring from her pocket and slides it onto her finger. She must have received the engagement ring during their own time together, in private, behind my back.

The choir sings, "Wonderful, Counsellor, The mighty God, The everlasting Father, The Prince of Peace . . ."

What I would give to see Appa barge in on this, wearing his clunky construction boots, with a bottle of Johnnie Walker in one tarred hand and a cigarette in the other, and kick the d-CON to the moon.

I'm the last to know. Judging from the way Lassie sits there, wagging his tail and glowing red among the tree lights, I suspect the dog is even in on it. He looks at me. The tilt of his head seems to say, *Oh, you had no idea? Are you really as dumb as you look? What's wrong with you? For your information, I'm in. You're out. Mung. Mung.*

thirty-four

Asa's apartment is packed with people. He tells me to wait. I stand near the door and watch him hopscotch over bodies on the floor and dodge the ones moving about. The Christmas tree is heavy with ornaments and blinks in red, white, and blue lights. On the door hangs a wreath made of red and green tissue paper. The TV is on loud. There's talk and laughter coming from the kitchen. I smell food cooking. An old man sitting near me says to another old man, "I'm walking and talking, ain't I? As long as I'm walking and talking, I ain't gotta worry about the little stuff."

A little girl with pine needles and crayons stuck in her hair comes up to me and stares. Her hair is a mess. A little version of Mickey McD. My fingers twiddle because two French braids would tidy her up in no time. She says, "What you got in yo' bag?"

I shrug.

"You got presents?" she asks.

I shake my head.

"You got candy?"

I shake my head again.

"You Asa's friend?" she asks.

I shrug.

"You Chinese?"

I shake my head.

"Then where you come from?"

I shrug.

"You deaf or something? Why ain't you talk?"

"Why ain't you shut up?" I say.

As soon as I speak the words, I want to take them back. The girl's eyes well up with tears. Her lower lip quivers. A pine needle falls out of her hair. She is on the verge of wailing. I quickly open my backpack, pull out a candy cane, wave it like a magic wand in front of her face, and say, "I'm sorry. I'm sorry. Please don't cry. Look. It's candy."

She takes my candy cane, puts it in her mouth, and sucks on it, plastic wrapping and all. When Asa comes back, she leans into him, hugs his leg, and tells him I made her cry.

"Why you mess with my fave baby coz like that?" Asa says, nudging my shoulder. He doesn't mean it. I can tell it's for show.

I make a sad face, pretending to cry. I knock the side

of my head with my fist and say, "I'm so stupid, stupid, stupid."

The girl laughs. Asa kneels down, hugs her, then steers his cousin back to her spot on the floor with the rest of the children.

As I follow Asa up the stairs to the top floor of the apartment building, I envy him, wishing for a crowd of family members in my home. I sit on the top step. He sits one step below me. Our voices echo, so we talk quietly. I look down at him and almost don't recognize the Asa Banks I know from school. He looks calm and open, not so tough, have-to-be-cool, and angry. I want to tap his head with my pencil, toss him some candy, punch his arm, and tell him my father died, my mother is marrying a thief, my life is in jeopardy, I myself am a shoplifter, and I'm going to run away and live in a tent, but instead I say, "Where's the money?"

He unties his right Nike sneaker, takes it off, stands up, and dumps bills and coins out of his shoe and onto my head. As I pick up the damp dollar bills and warm coins and count them, his laughter echoes in the stairwell.

"Man, you taking all my Christmas bread. Chill, it's all there," he says.

I stuff the cash into my pocket. I'm getting closer to the Shelter 365 and financing my great escape. At this earning rate, I may be able to ditch the talent show, but I'm going to need all the cash I can get my hands on, living on my own. I sit back down, take out a pencil and notebook from my backpack, and tell Asa to say the alphabet. He makes it to *L-M-N-O*, gets mixed up, starts over, gets mixed up at the same letters, and says, "Wait. I gotta sing it." He makes it to *Z*, but he sings so terribly I laugh.

"What you laughing at?" he says.

"Your singing," I say, trying to stop laughing.

He punches me in the arm.

"Your singing sucks," I say.

"Your mama sucks," he says.

I stop laughing, open the notebook, and say, "You are probably right about that. Can you identify this letter?" I point at *M*.

Asa knows all the letters, but he has a hard time writing them. He quickly gets the hang of sounding out short words like "cat," "rat," "sat," "mat," "cap," "sap," "lap," "mop," "top," "cop," "stop." . . . What he needs is practice.

"It's not as bad as I thought. You're not completely illiterate. You have a good base knowledge of the sounds the letters make. But you're way behind for your age. The only way to catch up is to read all the time, read whatever's in front of you. Not just books, but signs, cereal boxes, newspapers, posters . . . Sound out the letters, figure out the word, copy it down, whatever it takes. Start with the little-kid books and work your way to the harder stuff. Soon you won't even need to sound out the easy words because you'll know them just like that. You're smart. You're fast. You'll get it. You just need to practice," I say, and glance at him. Asa reminds me of a little kid as he sits one step down with his shoulders hunched over, looking up at me with a faint smile.

"Why you say your mama suck?" he asks.

"'Cause she does."

"That's cold."

"I don't care. Here, I got you a book. I want this read from cover to cover for the next lesson. Michael Jordan was checked out, so I got you Kareem Abdul-Jabbar. Do you know Kareem?"

"Do I know Kareem?" He says it like he's Kareem's mother.

"I'll bet I know more about him than you," I say.

"I seen you play," he says, and covers his mouth, trying to stifle a laugh.

"What was his name before he changed it to Kareem Abdul-Jabbar?" I ask.

Asa closes his eyes and says, "Oh, I know this. Don't tell me. Wait. It was, like . . . John something."

"Ferdinand Lewis Alcindor Jr.," I say.

He bursts out laughing. "His name was what? Ferdinand? That's a shameful name. That's worse than, like, Seymour or Norman or Oak Lee. Ain't you glad yo' mama ain't call you Ug? Then you be called Ug Lee," he says, slaps his knee, and laughs.

"Ain't you glad yo' mama could spell? Otherwise yo' name be like Ass," I say.

"Who you calling Ass?" Asa says.

"I'm calling you Ass 'cause you look like one, smell like one, and God knows you read and write like one."

Asa stands. He looms over me. He holds my head, his hands over my ears, and jostles it back and forth in his palms like he's handling a basketball before going for a free throw.

I push the top of my head into his stomach, and we tumble down the stairs. My backpack spills. Asa grabs my jacket and rips open a small tear on my sleeve. He grabs a handful of white stuffing and shoves it in my mouth. I bite his finger, grab his shirt, and stretch it over his face. He looks like Spider-Man. He punches me in the stomach. I cough and punch him back. We roll to the edge of the next series of steps, and I start to fall off. I think Asa will shove me down, but he pulls me away to safety. We tumble around some more, no longer really hitting each other, holding and rolling disguised as fighting.

A door to an apartment on the top floor opens. We freeze. A woman steps out and tells us to take it outside because the stairwell is no playground and what's wrong with you kids these days. "Is that you, Asa Banks? Where is your mother? Do I need to talk to your mother again?"

"No, ma'am," he says, standing up. "We apologize." He straightens his shirt, which is all stretched out. It looks like he's wearing a dress. I spit pieces of stuffing out of my mouth.

"Apology accepted," she says. Her tone changes. "Did you have a blessed Christmas, Asa?"

"Yes, I did. And you?" he says.

"It was fine. I got my grandkids here. They are a handful. The boy reminds me of you, Asa. You come up and play with him sometime, you hear?" she says.

"I will. Happy New Year, Mrs. Dorsey," he says.

"Be good now," she says, returns to her apartment, and shuts the door.

I pack up my bag. As I hand Asa the book about Kareem Abdul-Jabbar, I say, "Here, read it. And don't lose it. It's a library book."

He inspects the cover. "You know, just 'cause I'm a

bro and play ball, you think all I'm interested in is black basketball players? Man. That's wrong," he says, shaking his head and looking down like he's wounded.

"Are you serious?" I say.

"Did it even cross your little mind that maybe I wanna learn about some prominent historical figures, someone like Helen Keller? Did you ever think about that?" he says.

"Helen Keller?"

"Yeah, Helen Keller. That woman be deaf and blind and dumb. She can't see nothing, hear nothing, say nothing. And she still made something of herself. I know who she is, don't I? I know her name, don't I? Unless you're one ignorant son of a b, everybody know her name. That's crazy," he says, shaking the book in his hand. I can't tell if he's going to throw it at me or whack me in the head with it.

"Sorry. My bad," I say.

"I wish I had a mirror. You should see yourself. You look sorry like you shot your own mama. You going to cry? I ain't going to beat you up. You can't read my mind. You got no idea. You ain't that smart," he says.

"Kareem goes back?"

"Nah. It's all right. Me and Ferdinand, we going to get tight this week," he says, and pats the book.

"How about the library next time?" I ask.

"Nah," he says.

"You can pick your own books," I say.

"Nah," he says.

"Why not?"

"I got a reputation. Can't be seen with you. Can't be seen in no library."

"Well, I got a reputation too. I can't be seen with you," I say.

"Yeah, you got a reputation, all right. You Old McD's boy. She your girl?" he says, chuckling.

"No," I say.

"Look at you, Oak. Turning all red. That girl is weird," he says.

"You can be the biggest moron," I say.

"That's it? That's it? I just rip on your girl, and you ain't gonna lay moron me? Get it?" he says, and punches my arm.

"I get it, butt-face."

"There you go. You're okay," he says, chuckling. He gives me his open palm. I've seen him and his friends do this kind of handshake, but it's not a shake, it's more of a quick brush.

I brush my palm against his and ask, "Then how about the woods behind that old house?"

"You mean that creepy house? I heard a man shot up his family, then hanged himself in that basement and he be haunting the joint ever since," he says.

"Chicken?" I say.

"Me? No way. That's my dinner you talking about," Asa says, and gives me a friendly shove as he runs downstairs to his home of the four Fs: family, freedom, future, and food.

thirty-five

To excuse myself from church, I tell my mother I have two quizzes and a big history project due the next day. She doesn't challenge me. Lying to her about being sick would work just as well because she is in too much of a hurry getting pretty for the d-CON to check my forehead with her eye, which is caked with mascara, outlined in black liner, and shimmering with blue eye shadow. She leaves early because they're planning on eating breakfast at IHOP.

I borrow our neighbors' Sunday paper, looking for after-Christmas sales on camping equipment, namely the Shelter 365. I intend to return the newspaper. I'm merely borrowing it. They're probably still asleep. It's harmless. I am no d-CON.

The phone rings.

"I am bored out of my mind. What you up to?" Mickey says.

"Studying," I say.

"Boring, Goody-Goody-Two-Shoes. Why you always studying?"

"Because I want to get good grades, get into a good college, get a good job, get lots of money, get a good wife, get good children, be a success in the USA," I say, sounding like a robot.

"You don't need college to make money or get married or get babies. College takes too long. You know what you should do? You should open up a hair salon. You'd make a killing. I bet you could make millions just like that. You could be a millionaire. Guess what I'm doing right now?"

"You're on the toilet."

"No! Could you be more crassy? Guess again."

"You're putting on makeup," I say, turning the page.

"How'd you know? Ok, you know me too good. It's kind of scary," she says.

Safeway is having a sale on apple pies. Buy one, get one free.

"If you need to know what I'm doing at this very moment, I'm painting my toenails. My nail polish is all goopy and dried up, so I'm using Magic Marker," she says.

Peoples is having a sale on Utz potato chips. Buy one, get one free. My stomach grumbles. Giant is having a sale on Aunt Jemima pancake mix and syrup. I imagine a tall tower of pancakes between my mother and the d-CON, so tall it blocks their views of each other. The syrup oozes, mixing with the melted butter and coating the top pancake. It slowly drips down the sides. My mouth waters.

"Wanna skate?"

"No."

"Wanna go to that haunted house?"

"What haunted house?"

"The one you keep talking about."

"No."

Sears is having a sale on camping equipment: 25 percent off. The Shelter 365 is pictured in the advertisement. While supplies last. Even with the markdown I don't have enough money. I'm about ten dollars short. While supplies last.

"Wanna come over? My mama's here, but she's sleeping, and she going to be out cold until Timbuktu 'cause she worked the night shift and she going to be working it again tonight. She says it pays better. And my daddy, he ain't here. Not yet. He says he's coming for the talent show. Wouldn't miss it for the world. He says he's going to be staying a whole week. I miss him so much. I can't wait. And Benny's here sitting in his underwear with a jar of peanut butter, watching a preacher on TV. He's smearing it on his arms and knees and licking it off. It's disgusting. Oh my Lord Jesus Christ, now he's putting it on his toes, and Charlie's licking it off. Wanna come over?"

While. Supplies. Last.

"I'll cook you pancakes. My daddy says I cook the best pancakes," she says.

"Fine."

thirty-six

While Mickey cooks pancakes in the kitchen, while her mother sleeps, while Kelly watches for birds out the window, while Sabrina paces on the radiator, while Jill paws the pine needles off the Christmas tree, while Charlie waits for more peanut butter, while Benny, curled up on the recliner, sucks his peanut-buttered thumb, while the preacher on TV squishes his eyes together and prays, "Oh Lord, take me as I am," I sit on the couch within arm's reach of the sleeping mother's purse. It gapes like the mouth of a shark, the teeth of the zipper lining the opening, and it's full, full with a brush growing its own head of hair, a can of Aqua Net, wrinkled-up Mr. Goodbar wrappers, a pair of sunglasses, keys, a pack of Camels, a red lighter, and a wallet too fat to close, with a ten-dollar bill trying to get out.

The preacher prays, "Take me, Lord. Take me."

So I take.

thirty-seven

I pitch the Shelter 365 in the woods behind my father's dream house, which looks spookier than usual. I wonder if Asa was right about the man shooting his family and hanging himself in the basement. All those dead bodies. NO TRESPASSING. PRIVATE PROPERTY. The faded sign dangles on the trunk of a tree. KEEP OUT is spray-painted on the back of the house next to a skull and crossbones. Luckily, in the woods I can't see much of the house except for a corner of a boarded-up window on the second floor. The woods are dense with patches of shrubs among the trees. I crawl into the biggest patch and hollow out a space, cutting away branches and leaves. I pitch the tent and cover it with the trimmings. I test its invisibility by walking through the woods from all angles. It's impossible to detect.

I crawl into the Shelter 365, zipper it shut, and stock it with cans of SpaghettiOs, tuna, baked beans, and Spam in one corner, in another corner a box with silverware and toiletries, in the third corner a gallon jug of water, and in the final corner a stack of library books. Home sweet home. Outside, the wind blows.

I check on the Shelter 365 every day before and after school and spend most of my time there. I stock up on more supplies. I bring blankets from home. It's cold. And cans of green beans and peaches. I need fruits and vegetables. I need to buy more candles; they're cheaper than batteries, and they give off heat. It's cold. My place is getting cramped, but it's cozy. I need more money to buy more supplies. I leave the tent and return to the apartment before dark.

I pretend to be asleep when my mother comes home late. I figure she's been with the d-CON all evening, eating and drinking and planning their wedding and honeymoon escape to Hawaii.

thirty-eight

Mickey comes to school with a bruise on her cheek. She tries to hide it with makeup, but the black, purple, and green show through. I first think she's experimenting with using eye shadow as blush, but on one side? She appreciates symmetry too much to leave things lopsided, especially her face. When she sees me notice it, she says, "Why don't you take a picture? It'll last longer. Ain't you ever seen a bruise before? If you gotta know, Ma did it. She's accusing me of going through her purse and stealing her money, when in reality she be the one losing everything. I told her, 'Don't blame me. You lose everything. You lose your keys. You lose your jobs. And you be losing Daddy. You're one big loser. The only thing you can't seem to lose for the life of you is your weight.' That's when she smacked me. I can't wait for my daddy to come home. He's going to be at the talent show. I got a mind to stow away in his truck when he leaves this time. Wanna run away?"

"No," I say, and swallow hard. I tell myself that it isn't the lost money she got smacked for, it's her big blabber mouth. She needs to shut up. I have nothing to do with that bruise. It isn't my fault.

"Would you miss me if I disappeared, Ok?"

"No," I say, although I really would, but I have to be a robot right now.

"Yes, you would. I'm the only friend you got," she says.

"I have other friends," I say.

"No, you don't. Who?" she says. I don't say anything. "Oh, you talking about Asa Banks? You think he's your friend 'cause he let you play ball with him and his boys?"

"No," I say.

"Yes, you do. You think Asa's your friend. That's the funniest and saddest thing I ever heard. Be warned. He don't care a lick about you," she says. "Not like I do. I know deep down in that clenched-up robot heart of yours, you care about me, too."

"Dream on," I say.

"I don't know what makes you so mean and cold sometimes, but I forgive you 'cause I figure it's a broken heart you don't know how to get mended," she says.

"Shut up."

"Did I touch a nerve?"

"I'm not broken. You're the one who's broken. Look at your beat-up face."

As soon as I say it, I want to knuckle my head like my father used to do when I did something wrong and stupid. He'd knuckle me sharp and hard to knock some good sense into me, saying, "What's wrong with this one? When's this one going to become a human being?" I hold my face up to Mickey so she can take aim and punch me in the nose, but she doesn't. She bites down on her lip like she's about to cry, turns around, and walks away, leaving me feeling so much sorrow and regret that I huff and puff and clench my insides tight like fists, trying to turn it all into something else, like bricks, concrete, and steel, something that can never break.

thirty-nine

I get Asa on the phone. It sounds like there's a party at his place. He tells me to hold up. When he comes back on, it's quiet. He must be in a closet. I imagine him in the dark, sitting on shoes and being smothered by his mother's clothes.

"We've got to do this at the library. It's too cold outside, and you need more books," I say, not wanting to meet in the woods because of the Shelter 365.

"Uh," he says.

"I know you have a reputation, but no one is ever there. I go there all the time, and the place is a ghost town."

"Listen," he starts to say.

"You're quitting, aren't you?" I say. "I knew it."

"Hold on, what's that about?"

"It's too hard. You can't do it. You're giving up," I say.

"That's cold," he says.

"I don't care about you. I just want my money. You

cancel, you pay. It's in the contract. You signed it. You owe me ten dollars," I say.

"I don't have the money, man. And I'm not so bad with the reading now. I got the hang of it. I been flying through some books, man. I'm good, thanks to you," he says.

"Then pay me," I say.

"I'm broke like a dog," he says.

"Then go make some," I say.

"Now, how you propose I go do that?"

"You go to church, don't you?"

"Yeah."

"Take it from the offering plate," I say.

"Nah, that's not my style. I rather be broke," he says.

"Stupid."

"Who you calling stupid?"

"You, Asa. I'm calling you stupid."

"You all money drunk," he says, clicking his tongue.

"You're a stupid ni—"

"Don't, man. Don't say it. I'm warning you. You gonna be sorry."

"I can say whatever I want. You're a stupid nincompoop."

"Nincom—what?" he says, chuckling.

"Poop, Asa."

"Poop? Who says 'poop'? What are you, in kindergarten?" he says, laughing like he can't stop.

"It's not about the poop. It's 'nin,' 'com,' 'poop.' Look it up in the dictionary! N-I-N-C-O-M-P-O-O-P," I say.

"Yeah fine, Poop-boy, I will," he says, and hangs up on me, still laughing.

forty

Mickey and I are backstage. I didn't tell my mother about the talent show. It doesn't matter because she's never home in the evenings anymore since she started using the d-CON's kitchen to make her kimchi orders, because his kitchen is so clean and so big. She's too tied up with her engagement to come to a school cafeteria to cheer her son on while he stands still on the stage in roller skates, trying not to fall. Mickey keeps looking for her father. He isn't going to show up. But she looks so full of hope and faith, bouncing and gliding around in her costume, which consists of a red leotard and a flowing red scarf pinned around her waist. My costume consists of my mother's black blouse unbuttoned so low my nipples show if I don't stand up straight and the burgundy three-piece suit I got for Christmas, except Mickey said it had to be white, so she took a can of spray paint to it. The suit looks pinkish and fits stiff like armor.

Asa is backstage. He's wearing dark sunglasses and a black tuxedo, surrounded by his friends. He looks like Bond, James Bond. He ignores me. I ignore him. I have no idea what his act is going to be.

Sitting in the front row, ready with clipboards and pens, are the judges. I think they're all teachers until Mickey proudly points out Mrs. Larkin, the cafeteria lady, saying, "It's the miracle of hair and makeup." Without the white cafeteria jacket and hairnet, Mrs. Larkin looks like Queen Latifah wearing a tall crown of a hat covered in purple-and-gold snakes, and a purple leather jacket with shoulder pads pointier than the pizza slices she serves. When Ms. Bierman, the school secretary, finishes introducing the judges, she waves a big gold envelope at the audience and pulls out crisp dollar bills, fanning the money for all to see. "All the talented and hardworking students of Landover Hills are winners, but one will go home tonight with the prize. One hundred big ones! Break a leg, kiddos! Without further ado, ladies and gentlemen, let me introduce our first act. Sixth grader Mikoyo Kenji will play 'Für Elise' on the piano. Did I say that right? Is it 'Kenji' or 'can she'? Let's find out. Give her a warm welcome."

The audience applauds. The place is packed. I'm getting nervous. Mikoyo starts to play. It's the easy beginner version of "Für Elise," nothing impressive. A baby starts to cry in the middle of the song, so she hurries it up at the end. She messes up some notes. So it turns out that Miyoko Kenji cannot. It isn't bad, but there is no way her act is going to win. One down.

Second up is a dance group of girls from the seventh grade. They call themselves the Landover Hills Ballet Company. Wearing black leotards, buns on their heads, and ballet slippers, they sashay onto the stage and position themselves like ballerinas about to dance *The Nutcracker*. Until the music plays. "Can't touch this." The girls break out of their ballet positions and bounce in unison like MC Hammer. Everyone goes wild with applause. They're good. They got all the moves: the Running Man, the Cabbage Patch. They even throw in the Moonwalk. They're going to win. I want to call it a night, crawl into the Shelter 365, eat baked beans, and read a book by candlelight. Mickey's jaw drops. She's in awe. To make matters worse, the dancers end their act with a pyramid and the splits. If the judges aren't furiously writing on their clipboards, they're applauding and standing in ovation along with the rest of the audience.

A kid from our class does a magic show. It's a flop. Another kid sings "Amazing Grace." It's nice, but no one stands up. The cheerleaders crack up laughing, cutting their act short. They walk off the stage, pushing one another because someone didn't do something right and messed it all up. One kid tells knock-knock jokes as Ronald Reagan. He says, "Knock, knock." The audience says, "Who's there?" He says, "Gladys." The audience says, "Gladys who?" He says, "Gladys act is over, because I need to pee." We all laugh. He's funny, but not winning material. Then somehow we're up next.

Before I can tell Mickey this is all a mistake and I'm sorry and I do care about her and my father is dead and my mother hates me and is about to marry a bigger jerk than me and I'm going to throw up and run away, she grabs my hands and says, "I put some stuff in your jacket pockets. When I say 'fever' . . ." Ms. Bierman introduces us. The curtains open. "Stayin' Alive" starts to play. Mickey shouts, "At 'fever,' grab as much as you can and throw it out to the audience." I ask, "What is it?" As she skates backward, rolling me onto the stage, Mickey says, "Something to knock their socks off."

She parks me in the middle. I stand there, stiff and still. Mickey skates and dances around me. The lights are bright. I shade my eyes, and the audience applauds. Then I remember the robot. I hold my arms at right angles and move them like a robot. Someone hoots. I twitch my head back and forth. The audience cheers and claps to the song. Mrs. Larkin starts doing the Travolta in her seat. She glows. So I do the Travolta too. I can't skate, but I can point to the ceiling, hold my finger there for five seconds, point to the floor, hold my finger there for five seconds, and do it again with the other hand. Mickey spins, twirls, squats with one leg out, and scissor-steps, keeping the beat and smiling the whole time. She doesn't hold back. She performs like a real star. The audience hoots and hollers for her. It's enough to make any father proud.

Then Mickey goes off script and takes my hands. I don't know who is spinning whom, but we turn around and around, gaining speed, getting dizzy. Mickey's smile changes. Her lips curl and pucker as if waiting for a kiss. She wants me to kiss her right now? But her eyes are wide open, trying to tell me something. She is saying, "Fever!" Then Mickey lets go, throwing me to the front of the stage. If I don't do something, I'm going to roll off and land on Mrs. Farmer. I fall to my knees. Sliding to the stage's edge, I dig into my pockets, get handfuls, and throw them out to the audience. Millions of little white circles, the holes punched out of paper, drift over the judges, falling like snow. I toss out more confetti. With pockets empty and the Bee Gees fading, I open wide my arms. The audience stands up and goes wild with applause. The curtains close. We did it. Mickey and I did it!

Asa is up next. As the curtains open and Mickey

rolls me off the stage, Asa limp-struts to the microphone, wearing his tux and sunglasses. Some girls in one corner of the gym scream, "We love you, Asa!" Some girls in another corner echo back, "We love you more, Asa!"

"Quiet down now, girls," Ms. Bierman says.

He stands in front of the microphone, removes his sunglasses, slips them into his jacket pocket, pulls out a champagne glass, and holds it up. He clears his throat and says, "Ladies and gentlemen, I would like to make a toast, in the tradition of my family, who is here tonight, except for my ancestors, who are here in spirit, and my uncle James, because he needed to go see about a woman."

The audience laughs. He hasn't even officially started yet, and they're eating it up.

He takes hold of the microphone, presses it to his lips, and blows beats into it. It sounds like drums. Keeping the rhythm, he raps:

> "These, these, these, these,
> These are a few of my favorite things:
> The view from a tree
> A pretty girl's blush
> Making all my free throws
> A roller-coaster rush
> My mother's laugh

My father's van

It's big enough to take y'all

From here to San Fran.

My sisters sing

My brothers dance.

We gotta get up out of this trance.

They paved the way

They blazed the trail

Weren't in it for fame

Cannot be tamed

Say their names

Come on say their names.

When I say 'Frederick'

You say 'Douglas.'

Frederick."

"Douglas."

"Frederick."

"Douglas."

"When I say 'Martin'

You say 'King.'

Martin."

"King."

"Martin."

"King."

"When I say 'Rosa'
You say 'Parks.'
Rosa."

"Parks."

"Rosa."

"Parks."

"When I say 'Gan'
You say 'dhi.'
Gan."

"Dhi."

"Gan."

"Dhi."

"They stand beside us
They root us on
To spread peace and justice
from dusk till dawn.
Let's make the most
of what we got.
Life and liberty
Can't be bought.
Put down the guns
Let's talk it out
Give it more thought
No need to shout
Make the most
Of what we got.
Freedom to pursue
Happiness and love
Grace and forgiveness
Come from above.
So here's a toast
To you and me
Let's make the most
Make the most.
Make the most."

As the audience chants, "Make the most," Asa lifts
his glass, taps an imaginary one, and takes a sip of air.

The audience stands up and cheers. Some wipe tears from their eyes. Oh my God. He's really good. He's no nincompoop. He's a nincompoet. Asa Banks is a poet. No way he'll lose tonight. Even in my disappointment and defeat, I can't deny my admiration of what he accomplished. He made that up. He wrote it. It was genius. I feel proud of him. But I still need that money, and now there's no way Mickey and I are going to win the cash prize.

Principal Farmer announces the winner. It's Asa Banks. The place bursts with applause.

When I go to congratulate him, I stick my hand out and say, "You owe me money."

Asa shakes my hand and says, "Don't worry. I got you. Not now. Later, man."

I squeeze his hand hard and say, "No. Now."

"Not the time, man. Not the place," he says.

"Want everyone to know you can't spell 'toast'?" I say.

"Don't, man," he says.

"Pay up. Just trying to make the most," I say.

Asa opens the winner's envelope of cash, counts out ten ones, and throws them in the air. I catch two. The others drift to the floor. I pick them up, pocket the bills, and leave.

In the auditorium parents and kids search for one

another. In the midst of all the post performance pats on the back, I see Mickey looking for her father. Stupid girl. He's not running late. The plain and simple truth: He's not here; he's not coming. Someone needs to break the news to the poor girl. He chooses not to be here. It's not like he died and can't be here. It's impossible for my father to be here, because he's dead. Hasn't Mickey guessed by now?

As I make my way to Mickey, Lawrence Elwood, the new kid from Iowa, beats me. He taps her on the shoulder. She turns around. He leans in to say something into her ear. She leans in to hear it. She laughs, throwing her head back. He laughs, nodding too much like his head is stuck on a spring. I tap Mickey on the shoulder. Lawrence says he has to go and will see her in class. He hugs her.

"Pervert," I say.

"I think he's nice," she says.

"Nice like a perv."

She looks at me and asks, "Are you jealous?"

"You want to run away with me? We can stay at that house. You know, the one they say is haunted. It's not. I don't believe in ghosts. No one lives there. It's big and empty. Plenty of room for roller-skating. You can bring Charlie and his angels. It'll just be you, me, and our pets. I got some money saved up. Let's get out of here," I say.

"Be quiet, Ok, and keep an eye out for my daddy. He said he'd be here. He promised. He's tall, like over six feet, and he has a mustache, unless he shaved it off, 'cause I told him last time it tickled every time he kissed me, and he's probably wearing jeans and his blue Mack cap and he's real handsome and he might have a cig in his mouth if no one told him to put it out. I wonder if he stopped off to pick up a bouquet of flowers for me or something, 'cause he never comes to see me empty-handed, always has to give me a gift. He's got to be here somewhere. He said he's coming. He said he wasn't going to miss it for the world. Maybe there was real bad traffic. That ain't his fault. People get stuck in traffic all the time, especially when there's an accident or a broke-down car on the side of the road and you have the goodness to stop and help a stranger—"

"Shut up," I say.

"Don't you dare, Ok. Don't you dare tell me to shut up. Shut up yourself!"

"He's not coming."

"What do you know?" she says.

"More than you," I say.

"That is not true. You don't know more than me. You didn't even know how to skate before you met me. You didn't know nothing about cats and makeup and dancing before I humbled myself to be your friend. Tell me one thing you taught me. That's right. Nothing. 'Cause you don't share. You're sore and selfish. Don't go getting all high and mighty on me, 'cause you're not," she says.

"I hate you," I say.

"Oh my Lordy, you are such a crybaby. Just shut your ugly little mouth and stop feeling sorry for yourself 'cause we lost tonight. News flash, Ok. We didn't lose. We had a fun time. The audience was applauding like crazy. They loved us. We put on a good show. Look how happy everyone is. Life's not all about getting money, money, money. If you insist on pooping on my party, you can go run away and be all by yourself. I'm too busy having a good time and looking for my daddy to partake in your boohoo crybaby ways," she says.

"Hope makes people stupid," I say.

"Shut up before I smack you," she says. Her face turns the shade of red Crayola calls Scarlet. Then her eyes well up with black mascara tears. She stares me down, as if blaming me for making her cry. Now look who's being the boohoo crybaby.

"I'm out of here," I say, and walk away.

As I head for the back exit, I see a man who looks to be Mickey's dad. He has her eyes, set deep under cliffs of brows. He's taller than most, wears jeans and a Mack cap, and is holding flowers in one hand and a stuffed pink bunny in the other. He has no cigarette in his mouth, but when I walk by him, I smell tobacco. I know that smell. It's how my father smelled. I don't say hi. I don't show him where his daughter waits. I don't feel happy for Mickey. I walk by like he's another stranger.

Once outside, I run. I run fast and far away, feeling sore about Mickey's father showing up, her unbearable I-told-you-so happiness, about losing to Asa, about being wrong.

forty-one

Where were you?" my mother asks.

She isn't supposed to be home. She and the d-CON are supposed to be sitting in a tree, k-i-s-s-i-n-g. First comes love, then comes marriage, then comes Ŏmma with a baby carriage.

"Where were you?"

"School," I say.

She touches the lapel of my jacket and says, "What did you do to your Christmas suit?"

I shrug.

"Is this my blouse?"

I shrug again.

"Stop shrugging and answer me," she says, leaning in to my face.

"Yes, this is your blouse, and I had to paint the suit because I had a part in the school play that required me to wear a white suit and I didn't have one and I didn't want to bother you, since you're busy with the engagement and suits are expensive," I say.

"School play? What school play?"

"*A Ring of Endless Light*," I say.

"What's that?"

"The title of the play. It's about coping with loss and looking for true love," I say.

"That sounds so serious. What part did you play?" she asks.

"I was the priest," I say.

"Don't priests wear black?"

"That's what I said, but my teacher said I had to wear white or else I'd get kicked out of the play and get an F."

"What class was this for?" she asks.

"Language arts," I say.

"Did you do all right?"

"I think so. I had a few lines. I managed to remember them all and say them loud and clear."

"Why didn't you tell me you were in a play?" she asks.

"Because you're usually out with the deacon. I didn't want to be a bother," I say.

"Do you know what bothers me?" she asks.

"I don't know. Me?" I ask.

"When you don't tell me about something like this play. That bothers me. You disliking the deacon for no reason. That bothers me. Why don't you like him, Ok?"

"I told you. He tries too hard," I say.

"That's because he wants you to like him. He wants you to see him as a father someday. He's a good man. He's a smart man. He's a true man of God," she says.

"He's a thief," I say.

My mother looks at me, tilts her head, and demands, "What?"

"He's a thief."

She fists her right hand and knuckles the side of my head, saying, "What kind of human being are you? How dare you make up accusations! You liar!"

"He steals money from the offering plate at church," I announce, covering my head.

"Be quiet! Be quiet before I sew your mouth shut," she says.

"No. I saw him take the money," I say.

"You saw wrong," she says.

"I didn't see wrong. I know what I saw. He took money out of the offering plate and put it in his pocket," I say.

"You're making this up," she says.

"I'm not making this up. Why would I—"

"You never liked him. You never gave him a chance. Well, he's not going away. He's good for us. He's helpful. We need him," she says.

"I don't need him," I say.

"I do," she says.

"No, you don't. You just need money. I have money. See?" I say, pulling out Asa's ten dollar bills from my jacket pocket.

She looks down at the crumpled cash. She looks at me.

"Here. Take it," I say, offering the money to her.

"This isn't enough. What's ten dollars going to bring us? A box of ramen? A sack of rice? A bottle of lotion? It's not enough. It will never be enough," she says, shaking her head. She walks into her bedroom, letting out a sad chuckle and mumbling something under her breath about a silly, ridiculous boy.

forty-two

My mother and the d-CON talk on the phone. I press my ear against the wall, trying to catch the conversation. She whispers. She giggles. She whines like a child. I can't make out words, but judging from her unchallenging tone, I conclude she isn't going to ask about his thieving ways. I go back to bed and wait her out. She's on the phone for over an hour. Finally she hangs up, goes to the bathroom, and looks in on me. I close my eyes, pretending to sleep. She goes back to her room and shuts her door. I let an hour pass. Then I let another hour pass, making sure she's asleep.

At a quarter after two I get dressed. I layer on as many clothes as I possibly can without thickening my limbs so much that I can't move. I stuff my backpack with a flashlight, a bottle of ketchup, hot dogs, peanut butter, a jar of kimchi, all the Halloween candy I saved, and a loaf of Sunbeam bread. The girl on the bag, smiling at me while biting into a buttered slice, looks like

Mickey from one of her pageant pictures long, long ago. I hope she beamed this much happiness when she saw her father. I leave my mother a note.

To 엄마,

I am safe.

I have a house.

I have food.

Do not worry.

From 옥

forty-three

I walk to the Shelter 365. It's quiet out. I've never been up this late. The air is fresh. The crescent of a moon smiles in the sky. The stars twinkle. I can taste the freedom and independence awaiting in the promised land of Nobody Bother Me.

I walk. I whistle. A tune we were forced to learn in music class automatically comes out of me. "You'll Never Walk Alone." Mr. Bernardo made us learn that song by heart and sing it over and over again until he was certain we were singing with feeling and conviction. The song makes me wonder if I've ever heard the sweet silver song of a lark. Probably not, because the only birds around here are crows, and their singing sounds more like screams of panic and fear. I'm starving. I'm freezing. I'm alone. I'm scared. There on the hill stands my father's dream house. It looks more like a nightmare. Are those vultures I see perched on the roof? Are they crows? Or could they be larks?

forty-four

I crawl into the Shelter 365 and sleep. When morning comes, the light wakes me. It's freezing. I stay under the blankets, trying to go back to sleep because I'm not as cold when I'm asleep, and I'm in the middle of dreaming that Mickey is hugging me and crying black tears, and Asa, dressed in his tuxedo, is dancing onstage with a constellation of dollar bills and words orbiting around him, and the girls in the audience cheer him on, their hair done in French braids, and I dream that the d-CON, having swallowed thousands of silver dollars, suffers a terrible stomachache that renders him forever curled into a fetal position, unable to move, while my mother is speeding, driving my father's green Cougar through a desert under an orange-and-red sky in search of her son, and my father is standing on the roof of his dream house and looking down upon all creation, wearing a cowboy hat on his head and a tool belt around his waist and squeezing a hammer in his hand.

He smokes, inhaling from a cigarette, its tip glowing as it burns down to ashes.

I wake up. I light a candle and warm my hands by the flame. I try to roast a hot dog, but it takes too long, so I eat it cold. I open the tent and peek out. The coast is clear. I run out. While I do a number one, I hear shuffling in the bushes. It's a squirrel. It darts up a tree. I hurry back to the tent.

I tidy up inside. I do twenty-five push-ups and twenty-five sit-ups. The ceiling of the tent is spotted with sunlight that peeps through a tangle of branches outside. I wonder if anyone out there stopped to take a head count and noticed one was missing. Were the police called? Is the church praying for God to watch over the prodigal son, wherever he may be? Is Mickey running up and down the creek, calling for me, my name echoing through the tunnel? Does Asa dare to step into a library to look for me? I start to read a book. I take a nap. I eat a Milky Way bar. I eat a can of tuna. I have to go number two.

About ten feet away from my tent, I dig a hole behind a shrub. As I squat to go, I hear a cat meow. It walks near my hidden tent. It must smell the tuna. I pick up a stick and throw it. The cat looks my way, meows, and steps into the shrubbery. I throw another stick. The cat walks into my tent. I hurry. When I crawl back and look inside, the cat is licking the tuna can. It looks at me as if I'm the intruder. It has one eye. I know this cat. I saw it near the Dumpster that day I stole the lotion. I was running home, afraid of being caught. Seems like forever ago. I grab the tuna can. The cat meows.

"Hey, Cyclops, you want this?" I say, and lure it out of the tent. I place the can on the ground near a tree, and the cat follows me. As I watch it lick the oil, I stroke its back, wondering what Mickey's cats are up to.

forty-five

That night I run my trash across the backyard of my father's dream house and toss it through a broken basement window. Racing back, I feel like someone is chasing me. Maybe the man who hanged himself in the basement. I hear heavy breathing that isn't mine, footsteps that aren't mine, grinding teeth, and a voice that hisses, "Ready or not, here I come." I point the flashlight over my shoulder and look behind me. No one. Nothing. I dash back into the Shelter 365, turn off the flashlight, hide under the blankets, and chant "Jesus, Jesus, Jesus" until I fall asleep.

forty-six

I fight to stay awake in the afternoon. I didn't sleep much last night. It was too cold. Even with layers of clothes and a pile of blankets, I was freezing. I was shivering so much I started making plans for moving everything into that creepy house and making my father's dream of living there come true. Maybe I can set up the tent in the basement with all those dangling corpses.

The sun warms my face. I close my eyes. I can't let myself fall asleep right now, because falling asleep during the day means a night of being up, scared stiff and frozen under the blankets because of strange noises that sound like the swish of guillotines, heads rolling down stairs, ceilings creaking from the weight of hanged bodies, the gurgling of my mother drowning in kimchi, the thud of my father's body hitting the ground.

I yawn. My eyes become heavy with sleep. This is about the same time I would come home from school, eat something, turn on the TV, and fall asleep on our old couch, which has broken springs, cushions spotted with cigarette burns, and the smell of home.

I sit up and slap my face, telling myself to wake up. I throw off the blankets, unzip the tent, and crawl outside. The air is cold and sharp. I do jumping jacks to get my blood flowing. I do push-ups. I run in circles. I kick a tree. My heart races. I look across the field and see my father's dream house. It doesn't look so spooky during the day. It's just an old house. It just needs someone to live in it, take care of it, and turn it into a home. It's certainly well insulated with those overgrown shrubs. There's a chimney, too, which means it's got a fireplace. I am badly in need of a fire to keep warm. And roast my hot dogs. Dogs are not meant to be eaten cold; that's why they're called hot dogs. Light for reading. Conversations with the crackling flames. *Hello there, Snap-Crackle-Pop. Haven't we met before? My name is Ok. Nice to see you.*

I pocket my flashlight and scan the field for any danger. I'm moving into my father's dream house. The yard is clear. I drop to my stomach. I low-crawl toward the house like a soldier across a battlefield, dodging bombs and bullets.

I hurry across the cold ground, the steam of my breath leading the way. I push through the shrubs, reach the house, and shine my flashlight into the basement window. There's my bag of trash I tossed in last night. Cobwebs dangle from the ceiling beams. Rusty shelves stand along the far wall. On the bottom shelf there's a wooden crate perfectly sized to hold a colony of spiders or a dead baby or a creepy doll with eyes that open as it rises out of its coffin with knitting needles in its plastic hand, saying, "Who's here? I smell you."

I've developed some serious BO being out here on my own with no soap and running water. I'm not even sweating that much, since I'm freezing my butt off, but I stink. My breath is some kind of rotten too. Maybe my reek will scare off the ghosts. I move the light to another corner. I see stairs. No pale-skinned twins wearing white lace dresses sitting on the steps playing cat's cradle and saying, "Hello, we've been expecting you." None of that nonsense. The stairs lead up to the main part of the house. My heart beats fast. I'm scared. I'm excited. Feet first, I slip in through the window.

It's quiet inside. I shine my flashlight into the corners of the basement. I smell tuna fish from the can I threw away. No corpses dangle from the ceiling. No blood drips down the walls. No skeletal hands emerge from the concrete floor, grabbing for my ankles. This place is huge.

I slowly walk over to the metal shelves. They don't

mysteriously shake on their own, knock me down, and pin me to the floor. I look back at the window I came through. There are no clowns pressing their faces against the glass, leering at me. I peek inside the wooden crate. There are no bats fluttering out to bite my neck and suck my blood. Exactly what I suspected: empty. Nothing to be afraid of.

I breathe in the musty cold air, feeling dizzy and nauseous, wondering how in the world I ended up here, but there's no turning back. I move toward the stairs that lead to the main floor of the house. I stand at the bottom of the steps, shining the flashlight at the door, which is shut and covered in gashes that remind me of scars. It's freezing cold in here, but I'm sweating. I stare at the glass doorknob. Please don't turn. My knees shake. I hold the railing and test the first step, making sure it can hold my weight. I take the second step. The wood creaks. I take the third step. Then I hear scratching. My flashlight falls out of my numb hand, rolling down the stairs and across the concrete floor. It stops at the drain hole, casting shadows on the stained walls. I'm frozen. The scratching continues. It comes from the other side of the door. Slow and steady strokes. It sounds like sharp human fingernails against wood. The scratching grows faster, louder, and deeper. The door trembles. Too scared for fight or flight, I freeze. I'm paralyzed on the third step. I can't move. I shut my eyes and whisper, "Help."

I'm dead. That door's going to bust open, and a witch with nails as long as flagpoles is going to jump out at me and rip my heart out because she needs it for her chili recipe. Finally the door stops shaking. It's quiet. The scratching has stopped too. I hear a distant voice. It sounds like a girl. It's high pitched and whiny. It's saying, "Me oww." Maybe she's hurt. Maybe she needs help. Me oww. Meow. It's a cat.

I push open the door. It creaks. And there stands Cyclops. She slips between my legs, walks down the stairs, sniffs around, meows in judgment, and walks back up into the house. I follow.

The sunlight beaming in through the cracks of the boarded-up windows shows dust gently floating in the air. Except for the cat and me, the house is empty. I walk through the rooms on the first floor. More dust. More emptiness. Any appliances and cabinets, any signs of the room having been a kitchen, have been stripped out, leaving nothing but the imprints of what used to be. In the bathroom the tub sits perched on talons. The vessel is cracked and stained all shades of brown, reminding me of the Grand Canyon. It must've been a fancy tub once upon a time. The toilet's been removed, leaving a black hole in the floor. The sink was once fancy too, with its curvy edges, but it's now chipped and caked with filth and grime. I turn the faucet. Nothing.

Next to the sink is a door. I turn the knob, open it, and peek inside. "Ahhhhhhh!" I scream. I shut the door, back into the tub, and fall in, bumping my head against the rim. Did I just see what I thought I saw? I get back up and slowly open the closet door again and look inside. It's only me. Me inside a full-length mirror with an X cracked across it. No zombie closing in on me from behind with a knife in hand. I quick-draw my imaginary pistol out of my pocket, point it at my reflection, and say, "About time this town had a new sheriff."

forty-seven

The Shelter 365 is pitched in the living room. Its opening faces the fireplace, which has a fire in it, and in the fire is a hot dog roasting on a stick, which I slowly rotate so the skin evenly browns and blisters to perfection.

I bite into the hot dog and eat it the way it was meant to be eaten. Hot. It's so good. It's the kind of good that makes you forget your problems and count your blessings. So what if I took the Jergens? They got nothing on me. So what if I lied to my mother about the school play? So what if I took that ten? So what if Mickey got smacked for it? They can't find me. I'm gone. So what if Asa's better than me? Better words, better friends, better with the ball, better family . . . I don't care. I got space, while he's cramped up sharing a room with a village. I got my own place. So what if there's no electricity and running water? So what? There's a real roof over my head.

As I chew my hot dog, I take inventory of all my

food and water. If I ration and skip breakfast, I can go for about two months. I've got twenty-seven dollars, which is plenty for supplies to last me another month. That's three months covered. By then it'll be spring. Maybe I can plant some seeds out back. Maybe I can fix the plumbing in here, get some water running. Maybe I'll grow tomatoes on the windowsills. Maybe I'll grow mushrooms in the basement. When the weather warms up, I'll grow cucumbers on the roof.

A door creaks.

I drop the last bite of my hot dog on the floor. I dash into the tent and zip it shut. I listen. I hear soft footsteps. I peek out. It's Cyclops again, walking toward my tent, her tail meandering in the air like a finger wagging, *Naughty, naughty, naughty*. She meows, coming closer to me. She sniffs the last bite of my hot dog and eats it.

The sun sets, darkening the room. The beams of light disappear, taking with them the warmth and the floating pixie dust. The fire dies down. I don't have enough wood to keep it going all night, but this is warmer than last night or the night before that, and I crawl into my tent to rest up for tomorrow, because tomorrow I will need more food, more water, more wood, more strength, more ways to go on. It's quiet.

I'm about to fall asleep when I hear *scratch-scratch-scratch*. I pull my hat over my ears and bury my head under the blankets. I hear, "Meeeeeeooooooooow."

"Shut up!" I shout.

"Meow," the cat responds.

There's no way I'll fall asleep with that cat whining all night. As soon as I unzip the tent, Cyclops slithers inside and curls into a ball in a corner, cleaning her paws.

"Fine! Just this once, I'll let you stay, but you better be quiet. One meow out of you, and I'm throwing you out," I say, and crawl under the blankets. "No way am I feeding you. It's every man for himself around here."

The cat meows, as if to correct me that it's every cat for herself around here. She curls up next to my cold nose. Her fur is warm and soft. I'm so tired. I close my eyes. The cat purrs, reminding me of Mickey. I can see her roller-skating on the school stage. She looked amazing gliding back and forth in her red dress. She moved kind of like a flame. I meant to tell her she did a great job. I picture Mickey and her dad reuniting after the talent show. She screams with glee at the sight of him. He hugs her, giving her the flowers and stuffed animal. She hugs him back. She drags him around, showing him off to all the teachers. *This here's my daddy. Hey, have you met my daddy?* I hear her voice. I miss her.

247

forty-eight

I'm set. This is the life. I got a good fire going. I got a pile of wood next to me, a hot dog roasting on a stick, a good book to read, a one-eyed cat to rip on. *Hey, Cyclops! See this hot dog? Well, it's mine.* Okay, so I let her have the last bite. It's useful to have a cat around. Keeps the rodent population under control. The cat stretches and lounges in front of the fire.

I read about the heirs of Samuel W. Westing, playing the game of figuring out his death to win $200 million. I wish I had a chessboard. I wish I had someone to play with. I sure could use a checkmate.

There's a knock on the front door.

I freeze. I stare at the fire, trying to turn off the flickering flames with my mind. It crackles.

There's another knock, followed by slow footsteps across the porch. The boards creak. As the figure moves, the beams of light coming through the boarded windows shift on and off like search lights.

I quickly crawl to the front door and press myself against the wall, wishing I could sink in through the cracks and join the stains. I press my ear against the wall, listening for clues.

A thump comes from the basement. I know I'm not imagining any of this, because the cat perks up her head and meows. They're coming for me. I'm surrounded.

I'm about to dash for the steps leading upstairs when I hear, "Open up! Open up in there! This is the police!" Then I hear giggling.

"Seriously, Ok. Open up! I know you're in there. There ain't no hiding from me."

It's Mickey McDonald. Something in me cheers up. I feel relieved. I feel warm. I feel joy. I feel found. I hurry to the window and peek through the crack. There she is, wearing her raggedy green retro coat, her hair teased out high and wide like it's generating electricity.

"How'd you know I was here?" I say through the crack.

"If you trying to hide, you better turn off them smoke signals, Pocahontas. You letting me in, or what?" she says.

"Pocahontas? Really? Why can't you be nice and call me Geronimo instead?"

"More like You're Wrong You Know," she says.

"Man, I missed you, Mickey," I say.

"Knew you would," she says.

"Judging from your do, I see you got yourself electrocuted again," I say.

"Shut up and let me in, 'cause someone's going to see me out here and call the cops, 'cause I got a news flash for you, Ok—there's this 'No Trespassing' sign out here," she says.

"Everything's nailed shut. Go to the back. There's a basement window," I say.

"Shoot, I owe Asa a buck," she says.

"Asa?"

"In the flesh," Asa says, emerging out of the basement.

I want to hug Asa Banks, but I restrain myself and instead ask, "What're you doing here?"

He punches my arm and puts out his hand. I give him mine, and he leads my hand through a special handshake, something I've seen him do with his friends. He says, "Saving your badass self. Nice digs. Cool tent."

"Thanks," I say.

"Man, I need me a tent. I got no privacy in my own home," Asa says.

"I got plenty. You're welcome to mine," I say.

He looks inside my tent and whistles. "Now *that's* how you do it."

It feels good to have Asa's approval, but I try not to smile too hard.

"Hey, Mick's going to need help getting through that window," he says.

"Why? 'Cause I'm too big to fit through?" Mickey says, stomping up the stairs.

"No, 'cause you a delicate, fragile, beautiful flower," Asa says.

When Mickey reaches us, she takes a good look at me and says, "Oh my Lordy. You look like one of them poor Chinese babies on them UNICEF commercials. All you need is a bunch of flies swarming all over your filthy face, and people be sending you donations. What is that smell?"

"Hi, Mickey," I say.

"Hi? Is that all you got to say for yourself? Hi?" she says, pushing me in the chest with both hands. I fall back into my tent and land butt-first on the floor. "That's for scaring me to death. I thought you were dead! I thought you were mad at me 'cause we didn't win that stupid talent show. We didn't win 'cause of you, Ok, you and your sorry skating skills, or lack of, and 'cause Asa here played the stupid audience like a ukulele. Ok, I thought we was friends."

"Did you write that yourself?" I ask Asa.

"Hell yeah," he says.

"That was one lame poem. Didn't even rhyme," I say, standing up.

"Yeah. Maybe I should've put on some girl's roller skates and thrown trash at people," he says.

"Confetti, Asa. That was confetti. And they loved it." Mickey points her finger at him. Then she turns, wags her finger in my face, and says, "And you. Friends do not go away like that, and if they do, they pay the courtesy of saying good-bye. You are one rude little snothead."

"I'm sorry," I say, and put my arms around Mickey. She feels warm and soft. Her coat smells like cigarettes and shampoo.

"Oh my Lordy, get off me! You stink worse than Charlie's breath after he's licked his butt," she says, squeezing her nose and pushing me away.

"Sorry, but no running water here. I got dogs, though. Want a hot dog?" I say.

"Yeah," Asa says.

"No, I can't eat in this stink," says Mickey.

"I'll take hers."

As Asa roasts his hot dog, he says, "What's going on, man? Why you run off like that? Whole school be looking for you. All them girls asking when you coming back to do them dumb braids. Them girls' hairs is a big mess. They all be looking like your girlfriend here. Like they touch a live wire. 'Cause of you, I had to talk to Old

Mickey D, and you know I can't be talking to her 'cause of my reputation and all."

"Stop embarrassing yourself, Asa, and shut up," Mickey says, noticing the one-eyed cat in the corner of the room. She sits down in front of the fire and coaxes her out. The cat meows, walks over, and rubs against Mickey's knee.

"How'd you guys find me?" I ask.

"Your mom and dad, man. They be sick with worry. You know they come to school today and put out this announcement to everyone saying you gone all missing persons. Your dad, he be talking to the whole class, looking all businessman in his suit and tie. He made us bow our heads and pray so you could be found. Then we're riding home on the bus and passing this place and I see the smoke coming out of the chimney and Mick look over at me at the same time, and you know I never look at her on account of my eyes don't deserve to behold such beauty and all, but we know it's you in here," Asa says.

"The only reason I looked at you was 'cause you let out a big gasp so loud you had to cover your own mouth to shut yourself up. Man doesn't know the meaning of 'discreet,'" Mickey says.

"You pierce me, woman. But I do thank you for calling me a man," Asa says.

"That's not my father."

"Then who is he?" Mickey asks.

"He your uncle?" Asa asks.

"My mother's fiancé," I say.

"Then where's your daddy?" Mickey asks.

"Gone."

"Where'd he go?"

I shrug.

"What happened?" Mickey asks.

I look down at the floor.

"Did he leave y'all?" she asks.

I run the nail of my thumb along the grain of the floorboard.

"Did he pass away?"

A lump forms in my throat. My eyes water up, and a big piece of snot forms on the tip of my nose.

"Hey, Oprah, can't you see the man don't want to talk about it?" Asa says, chewing the hot dog.

"Of course he don't want to talk about it, but you can't not talk about it, or else you going to get sick in the head and end up camping out all by your lonesome in some dead family's living room."

"That's deep," Asa says.

"So when'd your daddy pass away, Ok?"

I wipe my nose with the cuff of my sleeve and answer, "In August."

"What happened?"

"He was working. He was fixing a roof. That was his job. It was a really hot day. And he must've slipped, lost his footing, I don't know, but he fell."

"Harsh," Asa says.

"I'm so sorry," Mickey says.

"That day? When it happened? It was around noon, and I was sitting at home by myself, watching *The Price Is Right* and blasting the AC. I wanted to go to the pool so badly, but I didn't know how to swim, and my father kept promising me he was going to teach me, but he never got around to it, and I remember watching that stupid show and seeing all those happy people jumping up and down because they won a new refrigerator or a new car, and I remember feeling so sore at my father because he couldn't get us nice things. The least he could've done was teach me how to swim. I was mostly sore at him because he'd yelled at me that morning." I take a deep breath.

"My daddy yells at me all the time," Mickey says.

"What your pa yell at you for?" Asa asks me.

"I don't know. Nothing really. Just the usual stuff. You know. How I'm lazy and all," I say.

"You? Lazy? I got plenty of words for you, Ok, but lazy?" Mickey says.

"Well, I was lazy because I didn't take care of something for him. He asked me to get him new laces for his boot because the lace broke off. He gave me money for it and everything, but I forgot. Well, not really. I didn't forget. I just didn't feel like it. It was so hot outside. Why couldn't he get his own laces? So that morning he couldn't tie his boot right, and he was really mad about it, and he left, saying something about, I don't know, something about a son being useless or something like that."

"Yeah, a daughter probably would've taken care of it," Mickey says.

"Man, that's so sexas," Asa says.

"What?" Mickey says.

"Sexas."

Mickey laughs and says, "Asa, it's not pronounced like Texas. It's sex-ist."

"No, it ain't, woman. It's sexas. I know this for a fact. Hey, Ok, help me out here."

"Who cares? You know what he means," I say.

"Oh, Oak here suddenly doesn't care about saying things wrong," Mickey says.

"Fine. She's right," I say.

Mickey smiles smugly and then gets serious again. "So hold it, Ok. You're taking on the blame for your daddy falling?"

The cat sleeps on Mickey's lap. She strokes her back. The small flame in the fireplace flickers among the ashes. Asa breaks twigs and lines up the pieces on the floor in a long zigzag. I bite my lip.

"Ain't your fault," Asa says.

"Yeah, don't beat yourself up, Ok. I'd tell you to forgive yourself, but there ain't nothing to forgive. You didn't do nothing wrong," Mickey says.

"I'm sorry, Mickey. I'm really sorry, but I have to tell you something. I did do something wrong," I say.

Mickey furrows her brow and tilts her head. I take a deep breath. "Remember that ten that went missing from your mom's purse?"

"What about it?"

"That was me. I took it," I say, and reach into the tent for my wad of cash. I pull out two fives and hand them to her.

"What?"

"Ooooooh," Asa says.

"I'm sorry," I say.

"I got smacked for that," she says.

"I'm so sorry. Here, please smack me. Smack me hard." I show her the side of my face.

"Ok, you are so lucky I am so full of pity for you right now. I don't want your money," Mickey says, pushing the bills back to me.

"Please take it. I don't know what else I can do. What can I do?" I ask.

"I'll tell you what you can do. You are going to return that money to my mother with a full confession," Mickey says.

"Justice served," Asa says.

"I can do that," I say.

"And I want my hair done for a year, whenever I want, however I want," she says.

"Cruel and unusual, man," Asa says.

"You got it," I say.

"And I want you to go back home, Ok. If you care a lick about anyone but your own sorry self, you need to go home to your ma and soon-to-be pa, 'cause they are worried to death about you," Mickey says.

"Yeah, they look real sad, especially your ma. She couldn't even talk 'cause she was crying and everything. You wanted bad. Go home, man," Asa says.

"I can't," I say.

"That's what you said about dancing and roller-skating. I'm not saying you're any good at it, but you did it," Mickey says.

"This here's cool and all, but you don't want to live here. It ain't home," Asa says.

"You don't understand. That man, that man pretending to be my father, is bad," I say. "He steals!"

"Judge not, lest you be judged," Mickey says, shaking her head.

"Amen," Asa says.

"He steals from our church," I say.

"And you stole from a friend. How you going to take a speck of dust out of his eye when you got a big old two-by-four in yours?" she says.

"Burn. Amen to that too. Time to put down your stone, man," Asa says.

"You don't get it. He doesn't care about me. He doesn't want me around. He wouldn't mind if I got into a little accident, if you know what I mean. Like . . . like whenever he drives me, he doesn't even tell me to put my seat belt on."

"My daddy is a professional truck driver, and he never wears it, and he never makes me wear it either," she says.

"And he nearly force-fed me mushrooms," I say.

"There ain't nothing wrong with mushrooms. I love mushrooms. My ma makes this one thing with butter and garlic, and she mix it up with some chicken and macaroni noodles. Man, just thinking about it makes my mouth water," Asa says.

"I always get mushrooms and onions on my pizza," Mickey says.

"I take my pizza plain with extra cheese. You try that new pizza place? They got, like, a dozen different cheeses. What's that place called?" says Asa.

"Da Vinci?" Mickey says.

"Yeah. Yeah," he says.

"I'm not crazy about their sauce. It's way too sweet—"

"People! The mushrooms could've been poisonous!" I say.

They both look at me like I'm crazy.

"Listen, Ok. You being out here on your own is more dangerous and life threatening than eating a couple of mushrooms. You're not right in the head," says Mickey.

"Yeah, I gotta side with Mick here. I don't know, Ok. Maybe you got it all wrong. The way he was carrying on about you, he looked like he cared. I thought he was your pa," Asa says.

"He was putting on a show," I say.

"Looked real to me, but if you say so. Look, I gotta head home, man," Asa says, and gets up.

"But you just got here. I have more dogs," I say.

"You need to get on home too," Asa says.

"Never thought I'd say this, but Asa's right. Go home, Ok."

"You guys are going to rat me out?"

"I can't speak for Asa, but I have a mind to 'cause I'm your friend and friends are supposed to care and I care and I'm relieved you're alive and I want you to stay alive."

"Stayin' alive. Stayin' alive," I sing.

"Seriously," Mickey says.

"I get it, man. You need to stop time. You need your own space. I know how that goes. But your ma's worried sick. She's having it the roughest right now, and I ain't no rat, but I'm glad Mick here is."

"Shut up, Asa."

"What? That was a compliment."

"I gotta get home. I'm supposed to be watching Benny," Mickey says.

As she hugs me, I say, "Thanks." Asa bumps my shoulder. I want to tell both of them, "Please don't go."

As the sun sets, the room darkens. The fire is out. With my flashlight I light our way down to the basement. I think about having to return upstairs without them, and the dread and loneliness hit me so hard that I stop in the middle of the stairs. "Go," Mickey says, nudging me. I proceed down. Mickey climbs out of the window first. Asa follows. I shine my light on them. They exchange insults and shuffle through the shrubs, making their way back home.

forty-nine

As I lie in my tent later that night, I blink my flashlight at the nylon ceiling, pretending I know Morse code and there's someone out there to receive my message. I think about Mickey and Asa's visit and wonder if they'll come back again. I should've told them to come over anytime because *mi casa es su casa* and friends are friends forever and friendship is magic and friends don't let friends drive drunk. Friends care. I remember Mickey saying I'm her friend even after I told her I stole her mother's money, and I keep hearing Asa's voice, saying how worried sick Ŏmma is and how this here is cool and all, but you don't want to live here. It ain't home.

I hear something coming from the basement. I turn off my flashlight and listen more carefully, wondering if Mickey and Asa are back. I hear footsteps on the basement floor, the *tap-tap* of leather soles. Those are not Asa's or Mickey's shoes. Those are not the paws of a cat. Those can only be the shoes of a police officer. It's that Jergens. They're onto me. They caught me. I freeze, my heart racing and my legs ready to make a run for it upstairs. The basement steps creak.

I unzip the tent, pop out, and scurry upstairs to the bedroom that has the loose board over its window. I lift up the board, squeeze through the opening in the window, and crawl out to the roof. The cold feels good. It calms me down. I find a nice flat spot, curl into a ball, and hug my knees, waiting it out. Tonight the moon shows a quarter of itself. I want to believe the moon smiles down on me, and the stars root for me, bringing light to my sorry heart. I press my eyes into my knees and breathe, telling myself I'm going to be all right, I'm not going to jail, I'm not going to fall and die. I lift my head and look down. Was this anything like my father's view? Did he have a moment to stop, take note of the thick heat in the air, the persistent sun, the interrupting butterfly, the rooted trees? Did he remember me? I rub my eyes because parked in front of the house is my father's green Cougar. What's Appa doing here? Has he come back?

"Ok-ah? Ok-ah?"

I hear my mother's voice. I start to cry because instead of sounding angry with me, her voice is full of sorrow and full of hope. She leans out of the window and speaks into the night sky. "Ok-ah."

"Ŏmma," I say.

My mother looks gray under the moonlight, like a shadow speaking to me from another world. She climbs out the window, crawls over, sits next to me, and sighs. She says, "I've been looking for you. I woke up one morning, and you weren't there, and it scared me to death. I was so scared for you. I was scared for myself. I was in a crazy panic and then all that frenzy and fear quieted down, and I felt my heart breaking. I couldn't eat or sleep or breathe, thinking I did something to make you want to go away. Maybe it was something I didn't do. I have so much regret. I hope you can forgive me. I see how you must've been hurting. And all I did was hurry you along, pushing you here, pushing you there, never once considering how sad you must've been."

"Ŏmma."

"Ok-ah."

"I'm sorry."

"I'm sorry too."

"I miss him."

"I miss him too."

"Was he proud of me?"

"Remember his walk?"

"He walked like a cowboy."

"He did. He walked so proudly, with his back straight

and head high. He had a strut. He never used to walk like that, not until he had you. That walk came from having you as his son. And here you are, living in his dream house, strong and safe, taking such good care of yourself. It feels good to see how independent and resourceful you've become. It makes me proud knowing you'd do fine on your own, but how I would miss you. I would miss you so much.

"I missed you, Ok-ah. I don't want to miss you anymore. It would make me feel very happy and very lucky if you would come back home. Do you think you can do that?"

I nod, my face wet with snot and tears. I struggle to breathe. My mother scooches closer to me, puts her arm around my shoulders, holds me, and says, "Our Ok. Our Ok has been suffering, hasn't he?"

I sob into her shoulder. She smells like home: my father's lingering cigarette smoke, the burned smell of the sewing machine, Jergens lotion, and kimchi. I gasp for breath and manage to let out, "You too, Ŏmma."

"I'm not going to lie to you: to live is to suffer. But it's just so much better when we do it together. Don't you think?" she says.

"Amen."

It's the deacon's voice. It snaps me out of my sobbing. He leans out the window and says, "Ok, I'm very relieved and happy to see you. You gave us quite a scare. May I join you two out there?"

"Yes," I say.

The deacon climbs out. Instead of crawling to us, he walks, wearing a long black coat, which, I hate to admit, makes him look like Batman. Just a slight resemblance. I want him to look more like Dracula, the bloodsucker that he is, but his eyes are too small and his skin doesn't look pale enough, and I'm feeling strangely generous toward him. I don't know why his appearance surprises me, since my mother can't drive. Who else but the deacon could've driven the Cougar over here? He brushes off his hands, takes off his coat, drapes it over me and my mother, and sits on the other side of me. I brace myself for a sermon.

He doesn't say anything. He looks out and sighs. The deacon's coat smells like cologne with an undertone of dog. My mother leans her head against mine. The three of us sit up here on the roof in the cold, looking out into the night sky. It's quiet and peaceful, and I feel a warmth inside of me that I haven't felt for a long time.

Then the deacon has to go and clear his throat. The moment was too good to last. I bury my face in my mother's shoulder again. Here we go with the sermon about how God created the universe, the moon, and the stars, and how he created me in his image and loves me so much he killed his only son for the forgiveness of my sins.

"Ok, if you don't mind, I would like to clear the air about something that I believe has been bothering you about me," he says, slower than usual, his voice sounding small and hurt. "It's about something you saw. It was on Christmas Eve. It was at our church. I believe you witnessed me taking some money that was not mine from an offering plate."

I nod.

"When your mother asked me about it, I was very puzzled at first. Then, I admit, I even got a little angry because I thought you were making things up about me. Then I went back and thought about it, and I remembered that evening. You're right, Ok. You did see me take money out of the plate. And you're right for holding that against me, because I certainly wouldn't want my mother marrying a thief either. But you didn't see the whole thing: You didn't see me putting money in before taking it out. I was getting change for a ten-dollar bill. I wanted to give the children singing in the choir some Christmas money, but I neglected to plan ahead and didn't have any small bills, and kids these days don't get excited about receiving loose change, and I wasn't going to give out tens and twenties. Anyway, it means much to me that I share with you my side of the story. Of course, it's up to you to accept or reject it. Your opinion of me does still matter, even though I've lost my chance at being a father to you."

The deacon speaks into the night air, his hands moving with his words. They open, close, shake, point, and rest as they animate his case. I check my mother's left hand. No engagement ring. Did she call it off? If she dumped the deacon, what was he doing at my school? What was he doing driving my mother over here to look for me? What is he doing up on the roof with us?

The deacon's shoulders are slouched. He sits cross-legged, balanced on the slant of the roof. His profile is blurry under the light of the quarter moon. His solitary figure looks out into the darkness for guidance and consolation from all those he lost, and for the first time I feel sorry for him. I feel a pity that makes me want to tell him how sorry I am and how grateful I am that he helped my mother find me, but I don't.

Instead I say, "You can make money singing in the choir?"

"Those kids are small, Ok," my mother says.

"If Ok keeps growing the way he's been, he'll fit right in next Christmas," the deacon says, and smiles.

Did the deacon just rip on me? I sit up straight and say, "There are a lot of great men who are small."

"Are they defensive, too?" he says.

Did he just rip on me again?

"I don't know. I guess Genghis Khan was defensive when he had to be. Along with Aristotle, Tolkien, and Gandhi," I say.

"How about Prince?" he asks.

"You mean the Prince of Peace?" I ask.

"No, Prince of the Purple Rain. You know, the Prince."

What? The deacon listens to Prince? I didn't see that coming.

As I lean into my mother, I feel a fatigue so strong that I briefly close my eyes. I hear her breathing. I hear the deacon say something about taking us back home. I open my eyes, look out at the stars in the night sky, and connect them, one to the other, feeling both great and small.

fifty

I'm on my way to Peoples Drug Store. I walk with the Jergens bottle in my hand. My palms sweat like crazy. My heart beats so hard it feels like a jackhammer pounding in my chest. I need to do this. I'm going to be a man about this. I'm returning what I stole and telling them I stole it. I committed a crime. I shoplifted. I'm sorry, and I'll never do it again. Confessing is the right thing to do. It's the only way I'll be free of feeling guilty and scared every time I hear a siren or see a police car. I'm nervous, but I'm ready, even if it means getting cuffed, arrested, and read my rights. Commit the crime, do the time.

The automatic door opens, and I walk in, heading straight for the checkout. The cashier chews gum, picks the chipped purple polish off her pinky nail, and licks her glossy burgundy lips, which remind me of plums. Her hair is in long cornrows. I wonder if I can strike a deal. I braid; you go easy on me. She looks up at me, her eyelashes thick and curly, like an army of commas. As she continues to attend to the removal of her nail polish, she says, "What?"

"I'm returning this," I say, and slide the bottle closer to her.

"What?" she says, and pops her gum, as if punctuating her question.

"I'm returning this, but I want to say something. I have something to say. I have to tell you this. A long, long time ago, it was a really long time ago, I . . . I . . . I . . ."

She rolls her eyes and taps her nails on the counter.

I stare down at the box of Life Savers and quickly spit out, "I shoplifted it. I understand if you need to call the police. I'm really sorry. I really am. I've been feeling so awful about this. So that's why I'm here today to do the right thing and confess my crime to you and return this and pay for it." My voice starts to crack. I can't cry. I can't.

I clear my throat and continue, "It's just that I was going through a lot back then. It's no excuse for my behavior, but my father had this freak accident and passed away, and my mother and I were left to fend for ourselves, and we were having a hard time. We were running out of money, so she was making all this kimchi and sewing and cooking and working as a cashier, and you know how little that pays, and her hands were dry, and she ran out of lotion, and I was braiding hair and teaching this bully in my class how to read better—well, he's not really a bully, he's actually one of my best friends now—and I was learning how to roller-skate from this girl so I could win this talent show that was giving away a hundred dollars in prize money, but we ended up losing, but it had nothing to do with her because she was amazing, and my mother met this holier-than-thou type of guy who just tried too hard to be my father, he kept taking me to the pool, trying to teach me how to swim, making me try mushrooms"—

"Ewww. I hate mushrooms. They're, like, the worst. Aren't they basically like fungus?" she says.

"Yes. Fungus. Gross. I'm with you. But I don't mind them that much now. They're not bad on pizza. You can't even taste it, but the guy asked my mother to marry him, and I couldn't take it anymore and kind of lost it and ran away from home."

"I get it. That's understandable," she says.

"I had to get out of there. But my friends tracked me down and found me and told my mother and her fiancé where I was, which was in a tent out in the woods at first, but it got so cold I had to break into this old abandoned house, which was also the house my father wanted to buy someday and fix up and live in. Well, I ended up hiding in there, but my friends found me. You know, the girl who taught me how to skate and the boy who needed help with his reading but ended up being, like, a great poet? We're friends now. We're good friends, and I was lucky they found me. I don't know how much longer I would've lasted, because I was running out of water and food, but that wasn't the worst part. I felt so alone. I thought all I ever wanted was to be left alone, but when I was finally all alone, I felt sad and forgotten, like no one cared about me. So I'm really sorry about stealing this lotion. I hope you can forgive me. Will you please forgive me?"

"Uh, sure?" she says, shrugging.

I hold my wrists up to her, waiting to be cuffed.

"What?" she says.

"Aren't you going to call the cops?"

"No," she says, lifting the corner of her upper lip like she's disgusted with the idea of cops.

"Thank you. Thank you so much. You have no idea how much this means to me," I say.

"Whatever," she says.

fifty-one

The old man's head is so close to mine that his bushy eyebrows look like they'll come to life and scurry off his face. He shakes my hand so hard my clip-on bow tie falls off. He mumbles something to me, slaps my back, and walks toward the deacon and my mother, who stand next to their wedding cake.

The hot July sun shines. A light breeze blows. Birds sing. Flowers bloom. It's lush and green in the backyard of First Korean Full Gospel Church. I sit on a hill and look out at the wedding reception. The grandmothers and grandfathers stand at the front of the buffet line, piling their plates high. Some deacons from the choir sing Korean folk songs, barbershop-quartet style:

"Just as there are many stars in the clear sky,
There are many dreams in our hearts.
There, over there, is the Paektu Mountain,
Where, even in the winter days, flowers bloom."

Ajummas from the fellowship committee scurry in and out of the church building, carrying platters of food. A man with his tie tucked into his dress shirt carries bags of ice to the drink table. Three boys, chasing one another, cut in front of him, and he yells at them to get out of his way. A girl throws off her shiny red shoes and runs in the grass. Her mother goes after her, brandishing a shoe in each hand. A group of fancy *ajumma*s stand in a circle, each with a Gucci purse positioned on her wrist; their arms are angled at ninety degrees. I can't hear what they're saying, but I'll bet they're gossiping. Still in his black robe, the pastor moves through the crowd, nodding at the women hard at work, shaking hands with the men, patting the heads of children, and smiling at the goodness of God.

The table is crowded with food. There are platters of rice, kalbi ribs, fried butterfly shrimp, bulgogi, japchae, dumplings, kimbap, potato salad, acorn gelatin, kimchi, bean cakes, rice cakes, crab cakes, sweet-and-sour pork, sesame chicken wings, spicy tofu, spinach with sesame seeds, boiled squid, pig ears stacked like fallen dominoes, pickled radishes, pickled cucumbers, pickled garlic stalks, and you got it, mushrooms, too.

Asa Banks is being chased by a bunch of little kids. He made the mistake of letting one kid touch his hair while giving her a piggyback ride, and now they all want a turn. His mom and dad stand in line at the buffet table, making their plates. It's nice to see them trying my mom's kimchi. They asked me how to say "thank you" and "congratulations" in Korean. I hope they try out their Korean on the deacon. He'll probably think they're saying some American words he doesn't know and look them up in the dictionary. That would be funny.

Mickey stands with a group of girls. Judging from the way she waves her hands, I'd say she's giving them hair, makeup, and fashion advice. Then again, she could be telling a knock-knock joke. She wears a dress she said she found at a thrift store for a dollar. "Made in Italy, Ok. It's vintage Oleg Cassini, Ok!" Mickey actually looks pretty stylish. Her hair looks great, thanks to me. Can't go wrong with a crown of braids. Her parents were invited to the wedding as well, but her dad is on the road, and her mom said she had to stay home and watch Benny. My mother said Benny was welcome too, but I guess they decided not to come. That's fine. It's hard going to parties where you don't know most of the guests, and Mickey seems to be having a fine time without them.

A woman with green eye shadow sparkling like a pair of emeralds walks up the hill toward me. She leans in to my face and says, "Tell me your mother's secret ingredient." She smells like French fries and Shalimar perfume. Her cheeks are streaked with pink blush like a pair of wings, and her hair is shaped like a big chrysanthemum. "Tell me," she says again, winking at me.

"I'm sorry, but I can't," I say.

"Here," the woman says, stuffing money into my pocket.

"Thank you, but I can't. It's a secret," I say, returning the money to her.

"Keep the money. I'm happy for you. You're such a good son." She puts the bills back into my pocket.

My mother's kimchi has gotten kind of famous around here. People from other churches order jars of it, and the Korean grocery stores stock it on their shelves. My mother puts a sticker of her smiling face and her name on each jar. She calls it Sora Lee Kimchi. It sounds like Sara Lee. Maybe she too will become a household name. Nobody doesn't like Sora Lee.

My mother stands at the bottom of the hill and waves to me. I wave back. She taps her fingertips on her mouth. I taught her some sign language after learning it from Asa, who's been teaching it to his entourage so we can communicate without teacher interference. *Eat,* my mother signs. With my fist, I nod yes.

I stand up, brush off the grass, and walk down the hill. I look up at the endless blue sky and assume a life of possibilities. As I make my way toward the party, Asa comes running to me with a string of laughing and screaming kids chasing after him. He gets behind me and grabs my shoulders, using me as a human shield to protect him from the mob of kids. They charge. I brace myself. I stand firm and open my arms.

fifty-two

I ride in my father's Cougar. It speeds along George Washington Parkway, his favorite road. It's lined with trees and runs along the Potomac River. It's dawn on a Sunday morning. The sun begins to rise. No one else is on the road but me and my mother. She drives my father's Cougar. She drives with only a learner's permit, no license. She is breaking the law. The black plastic bag of my father's ashes rests on my lap like a sack of rice.

"Are you ready?" she says, shifting gears.

I nod and roll down the window. The wind blows. My hair whips wild. My cheeks quiver. My ears deafen. I close my stinging eyes and think of my father, how he loved this car, how he loved to drive, how he loved this road, how he loved to speed, how he loved my mother, how he loved me.

I raise the bag to the window, open it, and release him to the wind, leaving a trail of smoke and ashes. "Appa! Appa! *Manse!*" I call out, my face wet with tears.

Acknowledgments

Many thanks to Michelle Humphrey at the Martha Kaplan Agency; the Maryland State Arts Council; Marion Young; Christopher Moore; Pamela Gerhardt; Regina Coll; Nicole Salimbene; Susi Wyss; Nan and Steve Cho; Julie Epstein; my editor, Reka Simonsen; my father, Sung Ho Kim; my mother, Linda Ji Kim, who makes the best kimchi in the world; and my husband, John, who works, cares, and dreams for me.